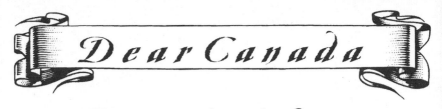

Banished from Our Home

The Acadian Diary of Angélique Richard

BY SHARON STEWART

Scholastic Canada Ltd.

Grand-Pré, Acadia
mai, 1755

Le 1er mai 1755

A terrible thing has happened. I have seen something I was not supposed to, and now I know something I am not supposed to know. I have sworn not to tell anyone about it, but my heart is aching. All I can do is write it down here.

I had crept out early this morning to collect *la première neige de mai* for Maman. Last spring there was no snow for May water, and Maman lamented the lack of it all year for treating sore eyes and ears. So this was my chance to win her praise — it is seldom enough that I can.

I scarcely slept all night wondering whether snow would come. But at dawn there it was — a thin silvery blanket over the fields and woods. It would soon melt in the first rays of the sun, but there is that glade in the woods where the snow lingers clean among the evergreens, so I set out with my bucket. Griffon followed me, as he always does, but I sent him back, fearing his great paws would spoil the snow.

Even in the glade the snow was going fast. I scraped up scarcely half a bucketful. Then I heard men's voices. One was Victor's! I peeked around a tree trunk and there he was. A stranger was with him, a tall and wolf-lean fellow with a hawk nose and high cheekbones. He was dressed all in buckskins like a Micmac, and a gun was slung across his back. He and Victor were shaking hands. I heard Victor say he would follow him to the devil and back, and that he would rally others to join the cause. Then he said the man's name — Beausoleil!

I gasped — I could not help it. For only one man bears that name. Beausoleil Broussard, the renegade who fights against the British. Victor has joined the rebels!

Victor heard me. In a moment he had pounced on me and dragged me before the rebel chief. Beausoleil has narrow eyes, cat's eyes, and he looked so fierce I thought he might kill me on the spot. But Victor told him the "spy" was only his nosey sister, and Beausoleil laughed. He still wanted to know why I was sneaking about the woods at that hour, though. I held up my bucket of snow.

Then he asked if I was going to let my tongue wag about having seen him, and suddenly his eyes were not amused at all. I knew it was not really a question. It was a warning. I crossed myself and promised to say nothing to anyone. Beausoleil nodded, then he told me to get myself home — *vite*!

I ran off, with my heart in my mouth and the bucket banging my leg all the way. I have hidden myself away in a corner of the barn to write this.

Plus tard:

Victor is furious! I have kept out of his way all day, but he caught up with me while I was milking Pâquerette. He demanded that I promise again not to tell. Why should I? Have I not already promised Beausoleil? So I just said he had better not stand behind Pâquerette when I was milking her, or she would kick him. And, *pour sûr*, she did. And I laughed. It served him right for being so bossy.

But, *hélas*, now my temper has cooled and I am very frightened. If Victor goes off with Beausoleil the British soldiers may catch him and shoot him! I long to warn Papa and Maman so they can stop him, but I have sworn not to tell. Dare I break my word to save my brother?

Le 2 mai 1755

I have prayed to *le bon Dieu* about what to do. I think I must say nothing, for did I not cross myself when I promised? So it is on my honour before God. Meanwhile, Victor goes whistling about his work as if nothing is wrong. Maybe he will change his mind. Surely he knows how much his running away would grieve our parents. But he is such a hothead!

A plague upon the British! If they were not here, we would not have these troubles. Yet Père Chauvreulx preaches often that it is our duty to obey them. And he must know. They have conquered our Acadia from France, after all, and our people have sworn an oath of allegiance to the British king. But Papa says we Acadians are sly like a fox, and that we can have our way most of the time and get along with the British too. It is a comfort to think we can outwit *les Anglais*.

Le 3 mai 1755

I should say something about my beautiful diary book. Its pages are thick and creamy-smooth to write on. It is the only really special thing I have ever owned. I had thought to keep it untouched forever and ever. Or at least until I am grown up and something exciting happens to me — up to now, nothing has. Except when the pigs got into Maman's vegetable garden and rooted it up. *That* was exciting, but not very agreeable. My ears still burn from the scolding I got. But now with this secret about Victor I am glad to have somewhere to let out my feelings. It is like talking to yourself, which I do sometimes, only better. It was Victor who gave me this book. He got it from a Boston trader last spring, and I loved it. I have been pestering him to look at it. So I was thrilled when he gave it to me as a New Year's gift. Victor is like that. Most times he ignores me, and he never notices little things he says or does to grieve me. Then suddenly he will do something *magnifique*, all of a swoop. And he always has a joke or a story to tell. Perhaps that is why all the girls from round about cast glances his way. That and his handsome looks. I do love him, though he makes me cross sometimes. I will pray to *le bon Dieu* to keep him from doing anything wild.

Le 4 mai 1755

In church today, Père Chauvreulx preached a sermon against sloth. Maman gave me many significant nods the while, and I squirmed in my seat. I felt the priest was looking right at me. I suppose I have a guilty conscience.

Through it all, Sausage kept glancing at me

with a smug little smile on her face. She never leaves *her* chores undone, of course. Maman always says she has more sense in her eleven-year-old head than I do in my twelve-year-old one. I made sure to tread upon Sausage's foot when we got up to leave. She hobbled all the way to the door. Zachary copied her limp. Claude grinned and Victor laughed. Maman gave all of us a hard look.

Outside, we stopped to pass the time of day with *les* Hébert. I noticed how Julie Hébert managed to stand next to Victor. She kept gazing up at him, and blushed every time he turned her way. She is setting her cap for him, that one! Maybe if Victor got married he would think no more of Beausoleil. But *moi*, I do not think he cares a pin for Julie.

Le 5 mai 1755

Papa and Victor and Claude are labouring in the fields today, sowing the spring wheat. It is late this year, with the soil so wet, Papa grumbles that now the harvest will be late too.

This pen scratches. Claude has promised to cut me a new one. It is good of him — Claude is never too busy for small kindnesses. But now I will have to go out and pluck a quill from Sergent — I dread that gander's nasty temper! I must make some more ink, too.

Plus tard:

I saw Victor talking with two of the Le Blanc boys down at the dike this afternoon. Was he telling them about Beausoleil?

Le 6 mai 1755

I am so excited! The date for Catherine's wedding to Basile Le Blanc has been set at last. Imagine — in three weeks my big sister will be married. It has been so hard for Catherine and Basile to wait all this time, ever since their first wedding date was moved when Basile's grandmother died last autumn. I think it will be wonderful to have a spring wedding for a change. Today Papa and Maman and Catherine and Basile and his parents went to sign the wedding contract before the notary. Papa and Maman are giving the bride and groom a fine milk cow, a ram and ewe, a pair of piglets and some ducks and chickens. *Grâce au bon Dieu*, they are rich enough to do so much for Catherine. We are all very proud. And I am very relieved because surely Victor would not dream of going off now and missing the wedding.

Catherine's marriage day will be *une grande fête*. And the best thing of all is that Catherine has asked me to be her witness at the wedding. I am to have scarlet ribbons for my cap, and a new skirt with red stripes. I never dreamed she would ask me. Poor Sausage is dying of envy. *Tant pis*.

Le 7 mai 1755

Victor is gone! He and Papa had a terrible quarrel yesterday. I heard their shouting clear out to the henhouse. Even *les Terreurs*, who were making mud-pies in the yard, stopped to listen. When I got back, I found Papa and Victor very red in the face. Maman was sitting bolt upright beside the hearth, knitting furiously. This alarmed me more than anything. She *never* sits down in the daytime — she is far too busy. Sausage was carding wool in the corner. Her big blue eyes were as wide as butter-skimmers, and brimming with tears. Sausage is so soppy! She cannot bear quarrels. Mémère was humming a little tune, so I suppose the loud voices did not bother her. That is one advantage to being a bit deaf.

Papa shouted that Victor will put us all in danger from the British. Victor shouted back that we are already in danger. That Governor Lawrence hates us because he wants our land for pudding-faced settlers from New England. That we have to *do* something, not just sit and wait to be driven like a flock of sheep.

I wondered what Victor thought we should do. I soon found out.

"We must fight them!" he cried. He said we should drive *les Anglais* from their new settlements. He said Abbé Le Loutre and the Micmac have been trying to do it, and Beausoleil, too. Suddenly Papa's voice went deadly quiet. He asked if perchance Beausoleil or some of his men had been talking to Victor, trying to persuade him to take up arms.

Victor shot a ferocious glance at me where I stood with my back against the door. I said nothing, but sidled over to the bench beside Sausage and picked up some wool and a carding brush.

Papa's face was set and stern. He said that Acadians have sworn an oath of allegiance, and must honour it. But Victor cried that he and other young men would not be bound by oaths taken before they were born. He turned toward the door. Maman jumped up and ran after him with tears in her eyes — Victor has ever been her favourite. He kissed her cheek and promised that he was only going *chez* Melanson to help them mend their stretch of the dike. For those *maudits* muskrats have been digging holes in it again.

And, indeed, he came back in time for supper, and afterward knelt with us all to say his rosary and receive Papa's blessing. But this morning his gun and his pack are missing and Victor is too.

Le 8 mai 1755

Victor's going has cast a cloud over us all. Papa is very angry, especially because there is still much work in the fields, and Maman blames Papa for quarrelling with Victor and driving him away. Claude says nothing. That is his way. But his eyes are sad, for he loves Victor dearly. As for Catherine, she mourns because Victor did not at least stay for her wedding. Sausage cried her eyes out, but then she weeps over everything, even dead mice. But Zachary is glad! He says now Victor will have adventures and be a hero, like Ti-Jean Le Fort in Mémère's tales. Boys are strange beasts, I think.

My own heart aches more than ever. Should I have warned Papa and Maman despite my promise? If something terrible happens to Victor it will be my fault!

Plus tard:

Claude found me moping in the barn, and we had a talk. I did not *exactly* tell him the secret, but he had already guessed I know something about Victor. Claude always notices things. I did tell him I had made a promise before God. He said that in that case I was right to keep it, no matter what. He told me not to worry too much about Victor. That he was a cat with nine lives — he could afford to risk a few of them. I gave him a big hug. Claude does not say a lot, but when he does it is *just right*.

Le 9 mai 1755

Today Maman seems more like herself, and I caught her giving Papa a kiss behind the woodshed. It warms my heart to know that she is not angry with him anymore. Maman says we must not spoil Catherine's wedding because of Victor. What would the neighbours say if we drag about with long faces? We have begun a whirlwind of housecleaning to get ready, and Sausage and I are at it from dawn to dusk. Maman overheard me calling her that name, and gave me a big scolding. So I have stopped — except in these pages. I say it silently to her sometimes though, just moving my lips, so she does not forget. But out loud I call her Cécile. I will not call her "Belle" as everybody else does. Even if she *is* the prettiest maid in all Grand-Pré, as Papa declares. It is a mystery where Sausage got her looks, for she is small and fine-boned and fair, not big and sturdy and dark-haired like the rest of us. And her eyes are flax-flower blue, not a proper Richard hazel brown. Perhaps the fairies left her. If only they would take her back!

Le 11 mai 1755

After mass Père Chauvreulx read the banns for Catherine's wedding. Outside the church, every-one congratulated Papa on marrying a daughter so well. No one said that Basile's father was mar-rying a son very well too. It makes me bristle! As if getting a daughter off your hands is like dump-ing a sack of useless chaff! Papa and Maman chat-ted long with *les* Melanson. It is the first time in weeks, for Papa and Monsieur Melanson dis-agreed about the boundary ditches between our best diked fields this spring. Père Chauvreulx and the notary worked out a compromise, but *au fond* they said Papa was right. So things with *les* Melanson have been cool lately. Today, though,

14

Papa and Monsieur Melanson shook hands warmly enough, and Madame Melanson offered any help Maman needed with the wedding preparations.

Jehanne Melanson and I fidgeted while the grown-ups talked. What a prideful creature she is — just because *les* Melanson were among the very first settlers at Grand-Pré! Jehanne and I are like cat and dog. I think *le bon Dieu* simply does not mean us to get on. Today she gave me a sidelong glance from under her black brows and said what a pity it was that Richards could not get anyone to marry them but Le Blancs. And I said that we married Le Blancs because they were such a fine family. I also made sure that she heard all about my new striped skirt and red ribbons. That will put her nose out of joint, or my name is not Angélique Richard!

Julie Hébert sidled over and looked cast down not to see Victor with us. Poor Julie! I cannot blame her for fancying Victor. What girl would not, after all? But she is past seventeen, and a girl that old should not wait forever. She will have to look elsewhere for a husband.

Le 12 mai 1755

It is most strange but now I have begun keeping this diary I cannot seem to stop. At first I meant to write down only important things. But now it has become part of me. I can write things here that I cannot say to a living soul.

Thinking about Catherine and Basile and Victor and Julie has made me wonder about Claude. Of course he would not marry for a long while yet, but is there a girl he fancies? Now that I have thought of this, it is like an itch that I must scratch.

Plus tard:

Well, I have my answer. I made an excuse to go to the shed where Claude was mending harness. I asked him what he thought about Julie and Victor. He laughed and said it would take a livelier girl than she to catch our Victor. Then I asked him straight out if *he* fancied any girl. He said that of course he did!

Now, Claude has never given the slightest sign of being in love. He never flirts as Victor does. So I thought this girl must be a sly one. I asked if she is pretty. Claude said she is very fair, though a bit broad in the beam. What a thing to say! I was astonished. Then Claude asked if I wanted to know her name. Well, of course I did! He said it begins with an "m." My mind was spinning. I thought of Marie Terriot. Or Marie-Anne Le Blanc. Or Marguerite Gaudet. But he shook his head at all those names. I begged him to tell me, but he said guessing was the price I had to pay for my nosiness. He said his love is a gallant lady, very fast, and he trusts her in all weathers. I thought he was joking. Then suddenly, I understood. He was talking about his boat, the *Madeleine*, which he named after Maman.

I flew at him and tried to box his ears for his teasing, but he just held me off, grinning. Then he crossed his heart and swore that the *Madeleine* is his one true love.

Le 13 mai 1755

Madame Melanson sent Jehanne over with a basket of preserves for pie-making. This was kind, for we will surely need them for the wedding baking. Of course Jehanne took the chance to snoop. Her eyes lingered on the unscrubbed pots on the hearth. Fine gossip that would be for Sunday, and it was my fault. I should have scoured those pots. Maman gave her some molasses cookies for her trouble, and slipped a jug of maple syrup into the basket. Jehanne smiled her sweetest, but as soon as Maman's back was turned I stuck my tongue out at her. I hustled her out the door and banged it shut behind her. Which earned me another scolding while I scrubbed the pots.

I have been looking over the quilt pieces I have collected. *Chère* Catherine has given me a piece left over from her wedding skirt for my bag. She must have noted how greedily I was eyeing the scraps. It is so hard to collect pieces, for nothing *chez* Richard ever goes to waste. Old clothes get cut down, or the cloth is unravelled and rewoven. Still, I have a good many pieces, and some are really fine. There is a square of scarlet stuff Victor got from a trader, and a bit of green-dyed linen of Maman's finest weaving. Maman also gave me a piece of an old waistcoat of Papa's all worked with her embroidery. Best of all is a piece of damask Mémère gave me — all that is left, she says, of a tablecloth brought by *her* grandmother from *la douce* France long ago.

I suppose it will take my whole lifetime to collect enough scraps to make a quilt. Perhaps I will be as old as Mémère before it is done. Though it is hard to believe I will ever be *that* old!

Victor's red square is like him — bright and warm. I rubbed it against my cheek. Where is he now, our Victor? What is happening to him? Oh, how I miss him!

Le 14 mai 1755

What a horrid day! First Maman scolded me because I forgot to scald the dishcloths. *Hélas*, I was dreaming of Catherine's wedding and threw out the hot washing water before I remembered. Maman said I was too old to be so careless. As punishment, she set me to stitch some pillowcases for Catherine's wedding chest. Mémère kept a close eye upon me. She made me pick out a whole hem and do it over, just because one or two stitches were a bit wobbly. As if anyone is going to turn Catherine's pillowcases inside out to check the stitches! Mémère made much of how straight Sausage's stitches are, and gave me a rap on the forehead with her silver thimble. Wretched Sausage giggled.

The whole day has been like that — one bad thing on the heels of another. I have had so many scoldings that I feel all in bits and pieces like the scraps in my quilt bag. But Griffon, who knows he is supposed to stay in the barn, has sneaked into the house and is lying under the table across my feet as I write, and that is a comfort.

I suppose Mémère only snapped at me because her rheumatism is bothering her these damp spring days. Usually she only shakes her head at me when I displease her. Not like Maman, who ever has a sharp word for me. In truth, Mémère and Maman are not much alike. But then, I am not much like Maman. It is strange how mothers and daughters can be so different. *Le bon Dieu* must want it so. But it is a puzzle.

Le 15 mai 1755

Yesterday evening, after supper, Oncle Paul and some other elders came. At first they puffed on their pipes and talked about boring things — the wheat sowing and whether the valve in our stretch of dike needs fixing this spring. But pretty soon Oncle Paul looked around and asked where Victor was.

Maman glanced up sharply from her knitting, and Zachary pricked up his ears. He always sticks his nose into everything. Claude was whittling beside the fire, and I noticed his knife stop as he waited for Papa's answer.

Papa leaned forward and laid his finger beside

his nose. Then he told Oncle Paul that Victor had gone after the wild geese. I was puzzled. Victor is not goose-hunting. Then I understood. No one will say Beausoleil's name in public. It might be dangerous.

After a moment a man said that one of the Terriot boys had gone off too. And he had heard tell of others. So my brother has convinced others to go with him!

Mother signed to Catherine to serve some spruce beer, and I helped her fill the mugs. The elders went on talking in low voices. Oncle Paul said the same thing as Victor, that Governor Lawrence wants our land. But Papa said that *les Anglais* have always wanted it, but still they have not taken it.

Then Monsieur Le Blanc spoke up. Now when *he* says something, people listen. He has just come back from Halifax. He says the place teems like an anthill, it is so full of British settlers and troops.

Maudit Halifax! The place is like a plague — people cannot leave off talking about it, worrying about it. I think it is a silly name. It sounds like a sneeze!

After the guests left, Maman spoke up. She said we still have time to find safety in the lands beyond the Rivière Mesagoëche — she is always wanting to move nearer her relatives. But Papa will never leave the lands he has worked so hard to win from the sea. At least, I hope he will not! He hugged Maman and told her that though the British may bluster, they never do anything. Maman stuck out her lower lip. She always does that when she is being stubborn. But Papa chucked her under the chin until she smiled. He knows how get around her.

I think I must have caught a case of Halifax, for my head is a-buzz about the British. It will be long before I sleep tonight.

Le 16 mai 1755

The weather has suddenly turned as warm as summer. It is wonderful not to have to bundle up to go outside. Behind the dikes, *la grand'prée* is hazed with green, for the new wheat has sprouted. The pastures spring with fresh grass and even our stately milch cows have turned frisky to be done with their winter fodder of salt marsh hay.

With the fine weather and the excitement of Catherine's wedding I cannot help feeling happy. But it is a different kind of happiness from what I have felt before, as though a little current of sadness runs underneath. Where is our Victor now?

Away up beyond Chignecto? Or perhaps not so far away at all, running through the woods with Beausoleil and the Micmac?

Plus tard:

Papa was down looking at the wheat, and he walked home with me when Griffon and I went to bring the cows home. He is so busy with the fields and crops that it is not often I get a chance to talk with him. I asked him if we would move from here, as Maman wishes. He laughed and said he would surely do it the day the tide stayed out. He winked, and I knew it was his way of saying never. He called me Pouliche, too. He has not called me that for a long time, and I thought he had forgotten his old pet name for me. I gave him a hug. Though I would rather be called Belle. But I suppose I *am* more like a filly than a beauty.

Le 17 mai 1755

Papa and Oncle Paul and Oncle Pierre have decided to drain more of our marshland for crops. I am glad, for now we will be even richer. But first a new stretch of dike must be built. Digging ditches and cutting turf is hard work. So all our neighbours will help. It will be *une grande corvée*. I asked Papa how long we must wait before we can grow crops on the new fields. He said it takes three whole years for the land to freshen under the rain and snow. Then it will yield much golden grain. Perhaps we will even get rich enough for Maman and me and Sausage to have new Sunday caps!

Papa says that in Canada the poor farmers have to cut down their forests and plant crops among the stumps. But we keep the woods *and* have our fields too. I think our way is much better!

Le 18 mai 1755

Today Père Chauvreulx preached about the sin of vanity. This time it was Sausage's turn to squirm. She thinks a lot about the way she looks, though she tries to pretend otherwise. I nudged her now and then to make sure she attended to every word.

Le 19 mai 1755

Just four more days until Catherine's wedding. The house is sparkling clean, but now we must cook, cook, cook for the wedding dinner. Pastries and tarts, sweetmeats and breads. And the wedding cake, of course. The rich *fricot* we will make just the day before. Maman always does it so. She says stew improves with a day's keeping.

Catherine does not say she is happy to wed, but I see it in her eyes. She has woven the most beautiful set of linen sheets to prove her skill. They are folded away with her other things in the carved wedding chest Papa has made her. And her Basile has made an excellent pair of wheels, to prove his right to marry. He brought them over yesterday to show Papa. He is a nice fellow, but I cannot imagine wanting to marry him. His nose is too long, and he never says anything funny. Yet Catherine seems pleased enough.

Le 20 mai 1755

Today I caught Sausage gazing at her reflection in the mirror. I could not bear the smug way she smiled at herself, so I gave her a good poke in the ribs. Of course she ran and told Maman, who frowned and told me I should be ashamed. She is right, but *hélas*, sometimes I just cannot help myself. Mémère says that if you let a baby see a mirror before it is one year old it will grow up vain. That must be what happened to Sausage, *pour sûr*!

Le 21 mai 1755

I am nearly at my wits' end! *Les Terreurs* have truly lived up to their nickname. They got away from Mémère this morning and tracked dirt all over the clean-scrubbed floors. Then they stuck their grubby fingers in the pies, trying to find out what kinds they were. A whole tray of sugar tarts went missing. Maman's patience frayed, and she had me take the twins outside while I did my chores.

Well, Marie-Josèphe swung on Pâquerette's tail while I was milking. Of course Pâquerette kicked the bucket over. Meanwhile Josèph-Marie chased the chickens. There were feathers everywhere, and it will be a wonder if we get any eggs for a week! Then Marie-Josèphe nearly fell down the well trying to see what was at the bottom of it. I grabbed her by her underskirt just in time. She burst out crying, and then Josèph-Marie bawled too, because he always does what she does. The only one who was happy *chez* Richard this day was La Gloire, who got to eat the spoiled pies. An ever-hungry sow is a great convenience.

Le 22 mai 1755

The apple blossoms are opening in time for Catherine's wedding. It is going to be so beautiful!

Tante Cécile has sent Cousine Geneviève to help us with the preparations. We had fun chattering while we worked. Geneviève keeps calling Catherine "the bride" in a sighing sort of way, but practical Catherine just laughs. Geneviève thinks weddings are wonderful. I am not so sure. Someday it would be nice to have a fine farm, *je suppose*, and for that you need a hard-working husband. But I do not want either one right now.

I am writing this early, for tonight is the first night of the wedding celebrations, and our house will be packed to the walls.

Le 24 mai 1755

It is daybreak, and I can hardly keep my eyes open. But I must write down everything about Catherine's wedding so I will remember it always. It was the most beautiful day. The waters of the bay were as blue as the sky above, and the red cliffs of Cap Baptiste stood out sharp and clear in the distance. We set off for the church at eight in the morning. Catherine and André Le Blanc, Basile's witness, went in one cart, and Basile and I followed in another. The carts were decked with posies and ribbons and there were bells on the horses' bridles. Catherine looked so pretty in her snowy cap trimmed with ribbons, and a red bodice and red-striped skirt. I was dressed the same, except I just wore my plain black bodice. Sausage had fancy-braided my hair with ribbons to match the ones on my cap. Sometimes she is not so bad.

As we jingled along, people were walking to the church, calling greetings and good wishes. We passed *les* Melanson, and said a polite *bonjour*. I gave Jehanne my sweetest smile. I knew she was not pleased to see me dressed up so fine.

Père Chauvreulx greeted Catherine and Basile at the door of the church, and we crowded in after them. Before I could believe it, they were man and wife. I wrote my name as witness, though André could only make his mark with an X. I am so proud that Mémère has taught us to read and write. We are fortunate that her mother taught her, and that her mother's mother learned her letters from the holy Sisters at Port-Royal. That was in the good old days before the British came to plague us.

The new-wed couple rode back together, so I had to ride with André. He kept peeping at me out of the corner of his eye and showing off driving the horse — as if Perle did not know the way home without his help! I feigned not to notice.

Just because so many Richards marry Le Blancs does not mean *I* have to.

All the neighbours trooped back to our house for the wedding dinner. It was warm enough to eat outdoors, and Papa and Claude had set up big trestle tables in the orchard. The grass underfoot was fresh and green and dotted with daisies, and the apple blossoms made a fluffy white-and-pink canopy overhead. Everyone ate and ate and ate.

After evening chores, we all met again *chez* Le Blanc for the *veillée*. Jean Robichaud tuned up his violin, zim-zum, and set our toes tapping. We danced and danced until dust flew up through the floorboards. I had André for a partner four times, but when he asked me a fifth time I said no and went with Jean-Baptiste Melanson instead. He is very good looking, but there is one big thing wrong with him, *pour sûr*. He is Jehanne's brother!

When the fiddler got tired, Pierre Terriot played the wooden spoons, rappety-tappety, and his brother Alphonse sang. The way he makes the sounds of all the instruments with just his voice is almost better than the fiddle. Later, Madame Le Blanc and her daughters laid out a cold supper, and we all stuffed ourselves again until we groaned.

At midnight, Catherine and Basile bade us goodnight and went to the room set aside for them. Zachary sneaked out and banged pots together under their window to give them a *charivari*, but Papa made him stop. We all went on dancing until it began to be light.

Such a wonderful wedding. I have pressed a sprig of apple blossom in this diary to help me remember it forever. But, oh, if only Victor could have been with us!

Le 27 mai 1755

How dull and quiet the house seems now that all the excitement is over! I miss Catherine. She never gets prickly like Maman, and puts things right when I do them wrong. And she never tells Maman on me. Not like Sausage. *Her* little tongue is always wagging, that one. Today I forgot to scald the milk pails and it was not long before Maman heard all about it.

Le 28 mai 1755

Today there was a *corvée* to raise a house on the Le Blancs' land for the newlyweds. It is going up fast — the wood was all cut and made ready last summer when Basile first asked Papa for Catherine's hand. The planks smell sharp and fresh, like new beginnings. Maybe I *will* get married someday. But not for a long while yet. And not to André Le Blanc.

Jehanne was at the *corvée*. That long-haired cat of hers followed her over, and Griffon chased it up a tree. I laughed and Jehanne was furious. That made me laugh the more. She went, all mealy-mouthed, to André Le Blanc and begged him to climb the tree and fetch the silly creature down. She fluttered her eyelashes at him when she thanked him, the bold creature!

Le 30 mai 1755

We have been so busy with the wedding and house building that I had forgotten the British. But they have not forgotten about us. This morning Monsieur Le Blanc came to warn Papa about a message from Fort Edward. It says that from now on, no Acadians from Grand-Pré may go up to Chignecto, or to Fort Beauséjour. Now, why? People go there all the time to trade and visit, crossing le Bassin des Mines and following the rivers. Sometimes they drive herds of cattle through the woods around the bay. We have cousins up there, too, beyond the Rivière Mesagoëche. Will we never be able to see them anymore?

Le 31 mai 1755

Chores, chores and more chores. And nothing but sharp words for my pains. It is not fair! No matter what Maman thinks, I *do* try to do things right. Or at least I *try* to try. But Maman says my mind is like a flea, always hopping from one thing to the next. *Hélas*, it is true that I like to daydream. I just cannot be practical all the time, as Maman would have me. She says learning to be a good housewife is a girl's most important duty. Maybe. But it is *dull*!

Le 2 juin 1755

Another quarrel with Maman. Must we be always at odds? Today it was because she saw me sweep the least little bit of dirt under the rug. It was only because it was such a lovely day and I was hurrying so I could be outside. But Maman was angry and said that I am lazy. And Mémère nodded until her cap frill waggled. It is a wonder how keen her hearing is when she wants it to be! Oh, how I hate it when both of them are cross with me at once!

I told my troubles to Pâquerette while I was milking. It comforted me to feel her warm flank against my cheek. Griffon pricked up his ears and listened as though he understood it all. He is *très intelligent*, I think.

Plus tard:

I have solved a mystery. This evening when Griffon and I went down to the pasture, I found Perle in a mucky sweat. I led her into her stall and rubbed her down and put extra oats in her manger. Claude had a look at her and said she has thrown a shoe. We searched, but could not find it. And Papa has not ridden Perle for days. Claude told Papa, and I noticed that Zachary hung about while they were discussing it. Then he said slyly that perhaps the fairies had been riding Perle. Not likely! As soon as Papa had gone, I collared Zachary and said I knew very well what he had been up to, but he just ducked under my arm and ran off, laughing. I suppose I should tell Papa, but I will not. I have wanted to ride Perle myself. She steps so lightly.

Le 3 juin 1755

The British came! Zachary and I saw red-coated soldiers ride by like a whirlwind. We hurried after them down to the church and found them nailing a proclamation to the door.

The officer in charge was yelling for the priest. People gaped at him, not understanding. But I did. Père Chauvreulx must have heard the fuss, for he came on the run. When he told the officer he spoke English only *un peu*, the officer flew into a rage. He stomped up and down with his face as red as his scarlet coat. For the proclamation was in English, so how could the people understand it? How stupid of *les Anglais* not to think of such things.

Then a boy stepped forward from among the soldiers. I knew him at once — it was Jeremy Witherspoon. He told the officer that he spoke French. The officer said he should tell us what was in the proclamation, and be quick about it.

So Jeremy read the proclamation aloud in French. By order of Governor Lawrence, we Acadians are forbidden to use our boats. And our men must surrender all their guns to the British.

Everyone began to mutter, and no wonder! The order is impossible. How can we fish and go about without our boats and canoes? And how can we hunt or protect ourselves from the bears and wolves if we have no guns?

As the soldiers mounted up, Jeremy gave me a little nod. He remembers me too!

Papa and Claude would not believe me when I

told them what the governor's order was. It makes me cross. They think I am a scatterbrain! And Zachary was no help at all. He was too busy staring at the soldiers to listen to the proclamation.

Le 4 juin 1755

Well, now they know I am *not* a scatterbrain. Last night Papa met the other elders *chez* René Le Blanc, and he came home shaking his head. He and Maman had words — I know, for I lay awake listening. It was the old story. Maman wants to pack up and move from here. But Papa will not go.

I have been thinking much on Jeremy Witherspoon and our meeting last year when British troops were still stationed here at the tumbledown fort in Grand-Pré. I had gone with my basket to collect wild herbs for Mémère in the big meadow above the east marsh. And there — *quelle surprise!* — was an ugly boy with orange hair. He had blue eyes, too. Not flax-flower blue like Sausage's, but pale and washed-out looking like a hot summer sky.

I took to my heels, of course. Maman has warned all of us against *les maudits Anglais*. But he yelled in French for me not to be afraid. Well,

I was not, really, for in my moccasins I can run faster than any boy. I stopped and looked back. It was strange to hear our good French language coming out of such a creature. The boy came closer, but stopped when Griffon growled at him. The boy told me that his mother had been an Acadian girl of Port-Royal who had married a British soldier from the garrison there. Both his parents were dead, but his father's regiment had taken him in as a drummer boy, to give him a start in life. He was not much older than I — I was eleven then, and he thirteen.

Eh bien, he helped me pick herbs and we talked a while. The poor boy was lonely among all the older troops. He had no friends his own age at all. I felt sorry for him. To be so lonely and so ugly, too, seemed very sad. When I had to go, he asked me if I would come again. I knew that I should not, but in the end I agreed.

I made excuses to go to the meadow several times, hoping that no one else would find out about it, for then, *pour sûr*, there would have been trouble. Decent girls do not meet alone with boys. But to tell the truth, Jeremy hardly seems like a boy to me at all — not someone a girl might flirt with. He is just an odd creature who became my friend.

We talked and talked. It was mostly in French, but when he found out I knew some English he taught me much more. It was interesting to talk to him, for he had seen the wide world — he had even been to horrible Halifax with his regiment. And then, in August, the fort was shut down and the troops moved away to Pigiguit. And I saw *mon ami* Jeremy no more.

Le 6 juin 1755

The *maudits Anglais* are back. Well, they are not all *maudits*, because I saw Jeremy among them. The soldiers say they want to go fishing, to catch eels to feed the garrison at Pigiguit. And they want to stay in the village overnight, two to a house. Papa is suspicious. He says the barn should be good enough for them. But no, they say they want to sleep close to the fire. What fire? It is so warm now that we do all our cooking in the summer kitchen!

Maman sent Sausage and me up the ladder to sleep beside Claude and Zachary in the *grenier*, saying she did not want us around such rough-mannered soldiers. At supper their eyes darted here and there as if they were looking for something. What can it be?

Le 7 juin 1755

We should never have let those soldiers cross our doorstep! At midnight they seized their weapons and ransacked our house looking for Papa's guns. They took every one we had! We have heard that the same thing happened in every house where soldiers were quartered. They are gone now, and the village is a-buzz. They took the guns down to the shore and there was a ship just in from Pigiguit to take them away. A crowd gathered, and in the hubbub I was able to speak to Jeremy. He says Governor Lawrence is on the warpath against us. Troops from New England are already at Fort Beauséjour!

What is going to happen to us all? And where, *where*, is Victor? For Beausoleil will surely join the French in fighting *les Anglais*.

Le 8 juin 1755

Even Papa is worried now. A messenger came through the woods from Chignecto with word of the attack on Fort Beauséjour. There are many troops from New England there and people fear the fort may fall — the last French fort near us. There has been no talk here about going to fight for the French, though. For myself, I am so glad that the news is out. I dared not tell Papa what Jeremy had said for fear he would ask who had told me!

Le 9 juin 1755

Papa and the other village elders are going to send a petition to Governor Lawrence, asking him to restore to us our guns and the use of our boats. They were drafting it *chez* René Le Blanc last night. Papa says they just want the governor to know that the Acadians of Grand-Pré are loyal whether they have guns or not, and that our lives will be too hard without our boats. Maman asked Papa if he would sign the petition. He said he would indeed, for he was no coward.

Maman muttered that *les Anglais* are like a nest of wasps — best left alone.

But the British wasps keep stinging us!

I worry about Papa and the petition. So many worries!

Le 10 juin 1755

For better or worse, the petition is on its way. Monsieur Le Blanc rode to Pigiguit to present it to Colonel Murray at Fort Edward. He will send it on to Governor Lawrence in Halifax. I saw Monsieur Le Blanc going by on the road, and waved to him. He tipped his hat to me, and I bobbed a curtsey. I felt very grown up. Jehanne was out by the road, but Monsieur Le Blanc did not tip his hat. Maybe he did not see her. *Tant pis.*

Le 12 juin 1755

Oncle Pierre came over to visit after supper. He said he had not signed the petition, and that if *les Anglais* make laws we do not like, it is better to ignore them and say nothing. Maman agreed with him. But Papa said that he was of no mind to try talking a wolf out of its dinner if it came after his sheep, and that he wanted his guns back.

I am proud of Papa for being brave. But I have a guilty wish that he had not signed the petition.

Le 13 juin 1755

Today Papa and Claude and Zachary sheared our sheep. The sheep bleated and struggled, and Claude and Zachary got red-faced and out of breath trying to hold them still while Papa wielded the shears. But once their heavy fleece was shorn away, the silly sheep seemed glad of it, and even the oldest ewes frisked like lambs when they were put out to pasture again.

Le 14 juin 1755

We washed the fleeces today. It always takes hours to get them clean, and a lot of thumping with a stick in a cauldron of hot soapy water. When at last they were cloud-white, we wrung them out and laid them on clean grass to dry in the sun. I thought I knew how much I miss Catherine, but I did not until we began wringing fleeces. It was very hard. I missed her strong arms as much as her cheerful smile.

Mémère overheard me complaining. She said I must look for good things to match the bad things in life. *Eh bien*, I will try. The good thing about washing fleeces is that your skin gets wonderfully soft from the oil in them. The bad thing is that you ache all over and smell like a sheep.

Le 16 juin 1755

Today was a beautiful day. A troop of us Richard *cousines* went picking *fraises sauvages* in Oncle Paul's big meadow. They grow better there than anywhere else. Geneviève came, of course, and Marie-Blanche and Marie-Madeleine came over from Oncle Pierre's. They are just as silly as Sausage is. Geneviève and I ignored them. We ate and picked and our mouths and fingers got all stained with berry juice. When we had enough berries for jam-making, we rested in the shade of the old willows that grow along the edge of Oncle Paul's land. Mémère says that the first people to settle in Acadia brought slips of willow from *la douce* France long ago, and they thrived here. A big one grows beside the fence in our lane — it was planted by Maman when she was first married. Whenever I am near it, I break off a twig and stick it in the ground somewhere else. I must have started a hundred trees by now!

Geneviève plucked a daisy and pulled off its petals one by one. At the end she pouted and tossed it away. I asked her which boy she was thinking of, and she blushed and said it was Louis Granger. Just imagine — Geneviève is only a year older than I am, and already she is in love. It made me feel queer all over. I do not think I could love any boy as much as I love Griffon.

Le 17 juin 1755

I found a fat rabbit eating the lettuces this morning when I went to hoe weeds in the vegetable garden. As it hopped off I told it that it was lucky Papa does not have his gun. I set to work, but I was daydreaming about Geneviève and

Louis Granger. Before I knew it, I had hoed up half a row of lettuces! By good fortune, Maman did not think to ask me how they are coming along.

18 juin 1755

That rabbit was not so lucky after all, for Zachary caught it in a snare and proudly took it to Maman. *Les Terreurs* were enchanted. They wanted to keep it for a pet. Maman said they had pets enough already. She gave me a meaningful look and told me to take the twins outside and keep them busy. That did not work for long. They wore me out with their nagging and crying to see "the fat bunny." *Hélas*, I knew Maman had sent it to a better world. But she just told them it had run away. They ate rabbit stew for their dinner and were none the wiser — no thanks to Zachary, who made a rabbit head with his fist and waggled two fingers for ears. I stopped him with a sharp kick on the ankle under cover of the table.

Le 20 juin 1755

Maman was right. That petition has brought trouble. Everyone has been hoping that the governor will let us have our boats and guns back. But no. He is angry with us. Colonel Murray at Fort Edward has sent word that all who signed the petition must go to Halifax to explain their insolence. But Papa and the others only wanted to make the governor understand that we need our guns and boats.

Oh, I hope he does not go to horrible Halifax!

Le 21 juin 1755

Papa and the others are going to draw up a new petition, telling the governor they did not mean to anger him, but only to explain about the guns and boats. All the same people will sign it as did before. Maman stuck out her lip when Papa told her, and said he was a fool to sign again. Papa stroked her hair and soothed her as if she were Marie-Josèphe, saying that it would be wrong to break faith with the others. I suppose he is right, but still I wish he would not sign.

Le 23 juin 1755

Fort Beauséjour has fallen! Papa's face turned grey as ashes when he heard the news, and he said that now *les Anglais* have nothing more to fear. Maman crossed herself.

I asked Papa what the British wanted with Fort

Beauséjour when they already had their own fort right across the river from it. He said they mean to drive the French all the way back to Canada if they can. I asked if they would drive us out, too, for are we not French? But he said they would not, for we do not fight them.

But Victor does! And after all the worries *les Anglais* are causing us, I have a sneaking wish that I could, too!

Le 24 juin 1755

We have a secret visitor! Tonight a distant cousin of Maman arrived from Chignecto. He came through the woods and paddled a canoe across the bay after dark. Griffon went wild barking in the night, and when Papa went out to quiet him, he found Bernard à Mathurin. Papa has agreed to hide him up in the *grenier* if the British come. Papa and Maman call him Bernard à Mathurin, because he is a son of Mathurin Daigle, a cousin of Maman's. He and his family moved across the Rivière Mesagoëche to start a new life away from *les Anglais* years ago. *Moi*, I do not remember these cousins at all. I suppose I was too little when they went away.

Bernard à Mathurin wolfed down three bowls

of Maman's *fricot* without stopping. He said he had to travel secretly and not make cooking fires along the way, for fear the British would catch him. He was near Beauséjour when the French commander surrendered. That was the day we went berry picking. How awful that people were fighting and dying while Geneviève and I were stuffing ourselves with strawberries and talking of love!

Our cousin says there must have been treachery for the fort to fall so soon. Even worse, when the British marched in, they found many Acadian men inside who had been fighting with the French. No one knows what the British will do to them.

When Maman heard that, she gasped. Sausage was standing beside me, and she slipped her hand into mine. It was like a lump of ice. We were all afraid Victor might be among the men captured. But then Bernard à Mathurin said that while the British were busy at the fort, Beausoleil and his men fell upon their camp and destroyed it.

I felt a fierce, hot feeling I have never known before. I am glad our men struck back! Victor must be with Beausoleil, *pour sûr*, and not locked up in prison after all. Oh, how I hope so!

Le 25 juin 1755

They have sent the second petition. May it turn aside the governor's wrath, so that Papa does not have to go away. I tremble to think how worried and frightened we would be without him.

Le 26 juin 1755

Bernard à Mathurin has left us to go to his relatives in Pigiguit. We go about our chores under a cloud of worry. Though the weather is fair and fine, we cannot enjoy it. *Les Anglais* are even spoiling the summer for us!

Le 28 juin 1755

More bad news! We have heard that the governor is still angry. Papa and the others must go to Halifax to face him. What will he do to them? Maybe he will shoot them!

I am out of patience with Zachary! The little wretch cares for nothing but adventures. He thinks it is a fine thing for Papa to go to Halifax, and pesters him to bring presents when he comes back. I told him to bite his tongue. But he just stuck it out at me.

Le 29 juin 1755

Maman has fretted and fussed at Papa for days, blaming him for signing the petition. What is the use? I wish he had not, too. But what is done is done. Yet now that Papa must go to Halifax, she is perfectly calm. She has packed his things and we are preparing a good hamper of food for him to take with him. Sausage helped me make Papa's favourite *tourtière*, the kind we usually make for Christmas, to comfort him. Papa gave us both a hug when he saw it. Sausage burst into sobs, and clung to him, but he told her she must not spoil the bluest eyes in all Acadia with tears. He said that he and Governor Lawrence might get along very well, and that he might offer him a piece of our famous pie.

But he looked at me over the top of her head, and his eyes were not merry at all.

Le 30 juin 1755

Papa is gone. He and the others are on their way to Halifax. Maman has not forgiven him about the petition. I could tell by the way she bade him goodbye, just offering him her cheek to kiss. Why must she be so stubborn? *Moi*, I gave him a hearty smack. At the last, Papa took me aside and told me to be good to Maman. He called me Angélique, not Pouliche, so I knew he meant it seriously. I suppose he has noticed that we are always quarrelling. I will try not to from now on. We all followed the riders down the road a good way, but at last we had to turn back. Just before he disappeared into the woods, Papa swept off his hat and waved it at us.

May *le bon Dieu* protect Papa! Our home feels strange — hollow — without him.

Le 1ᵉʳ juillet 1755

I have been reading over this diary. Real trouble makes me see what a foolish girl I have been. Bored when nothing interesting happens. Groaning over chores. Cross with Maman when she casts up my lazy ways to me, and envious because Sausage is prettier that I am. *Mais, non*! I will not call her Sausage anymore, not even in these pages. I will not even call her Cécile. Our dear papa calls her Belle, and from now on I will, too.

Le 2 juillet 1755

I comfort myself that Papa may not even have reached Halifax. So we need not worry too much about him yet. I told this to Belle, when I caught her weeping into the bread dough. But it did not cheer her up. So I told her Papa's saying that Acadians are sly as the fox, and said that our menfolk will surely get around the stupid governor. That made her smile a little. I wish I could believe it myself! Because — I will admit it only here — I am very, very frightened for Papa. But I know he would want me to be brave like him. So I try.

Le 3 juillet 1755

The pot herbs in Maman's garden are so well-grown that Mémère said we must begin to cut and salt them. As if there is not enough to do with the work of the house and the barn! And it is a finicking task. We put up two jars of chopped chives, savory and chervil, all layered with coarse salt.

Here I am wasting ink and paper on complaints again!

Le 4 juillet 1755

That Zachary! Today he ran off leaving his chores undone. At first we thought he might be with Claude and the others working on the dike, but when Belle ran down to ask, Claude had not seen him. With Papa away, Zachary is getting quite wild. So it fell to me to do all my chores and his, too. I do hate mucking out the stables. But Belle came and helped me, though she had the whole vegetable garden to tend as well as her housework. Her kindness shames me when I think on the nasty things I used to say to her.

Plus tard:

Zachary came whistling home with a string of fine trout from the Rivière Gaspereau. He was very pleased with himself, and seemed quite surprised that we were all angry with him. Still, some of the fish made a tasty supper, and we built a slow fire of wood chips in the smokehouse to cure the rest. Papa loves smoked trout — it will be a treat for him when he gets back.

Belle and I had our revenge on Zachary: while he was gone we tied all his bedclothes into the fanciest knots we could think of to pay him back. And I tucked in a few burrs and stinging nettles for good measure. After he climbed up to the *grenier* to go to bed there was a lot of yelping and thumping, and we could hear Claude laughing.

Le 5 juillet 1755

Papa will certainly be in Halifax by now. The thought of that hangs over us like a black cloud. Maman thinks of a thousand extra things for Belle and me to do. It is irksome. I suspect she does it to keep us from fretting. It does not.

Today she set us to butter-making. Now, usually Maman says lard is better for everything, and likes to use the creamy-rich milk in her cooking. But today she suddenly decided she had to have butter. We poured the cream into the churn and thumped the dasher until our arms ached. Still no butter. More thumping. It was hot work, too, even in the cool dairy. The longer it went on, the more vengeful my thumps became. Belle laughed and said that without my temper we might have been at it all day.

At last the wretched butter got itself together, and we patted it into moulds. There was plenty of buttermilk left over. Belle loves to drink it. She kept a bit over to wash her face, too. Mémère says it is good for the complexion. *Moi*, I think buttermilk is disgusting. The lumps of fat in it make my stomach roil. So I poured my share into La Gloire's trough. *She* will eat anything.

Le 7 juillet 1755

Today Maman sent me with barley water to the men working on the dike. The bucket was too heavy for Belle, and Zachary would have managed to spill the water before he got there. Griffon and I took the path along the top of the dike. The tide was out, and the mud flats smelled stinky-salty the way they always do. I love to watch the sandpipers patter about on their queer stilt-like legs, pecking out food.

The men were glad enough to lay down their tools and take a cool drink. Claude sat beside me on top of the dike while I waited for them finish. His eyes gazed far away, where the wind was whipping the waters of the bay into stiff white-caps. I suspect he was thinking of the *Madeleine*. He must be missing her now that the British have forbidden us to use our boats. For my brother's heart always yearns for the sea.

In the summer, he often works on French or New England fishing boats to fill in the time between planting and harvest. He always comes home sun-browned and content, with money in his pocket and a look in his eyes that tells of far-away places. But there will be no journeys this summer — not with Victor gone and Papa in

Halifax. Now he has to do their work as well as his own. *Pauvre* Claude! Yet he never complains. Not like me.

Le 8 juillet 1755

I try not to wonder too much about Papa, but I cannot help it. And I worry about Victor, too. What will happen to Beausoleil and his men now that the British have won? Will they still keep on fighting? Or might Victor come home? Oh, how wonderful that would be.

Le 10 juillet 1755

As if we do not have enough trouble! Now Reine has broken her leg and has had to be put down. And it is Zachary's fault. The poor cow got stuck in the mud at the edge of a ditch in the pasture. Zachary found her when he went to bring in the herd. If he had let her alone and gone for help, she could have been dug out. But no, he had to try to scare her into jerking herself free. She snapped her leg, and Claude had to put her out of her misery. Now we must have a *boucherie*, and be quick about it, for the meat will not keep in warm weather.

Le 11 juillet 1755

All our neighbours round about came for the *boucherie*. It was like magic how they knew we needed help. The men set to work and the carcass was skinned and butchered in no time. Maman told me to keep *les Terreurs* away from the gory sight. As well try to keep water in a sieve! They scampered about and got in everyone's way. The men scraped and treated the hide. Papa will make moccasins and boots for us all from it next winter. Meanwhile, the women helped Maman and Belle and Catherine and me turn our poor cow into cuts for braising and stewing. She would be much too tough for roasting.

We gave the workers a good *ragoût* for their dinner, but the twins, who had loved the excitement of the *boucherie*, suddenly realized their dinner was poor Reine. They began to wail and would not eat a mouthful. Belle comforted them with bread and lard and maple sugar.

After dinner was eaten there was a frolic. Our best fiddler is in Halifax with Papa and the others, but his son played for us. A few young couples danced, but nobody's heart was really in it, not like the *veillée* after Catherine's wedding. At last everyone went home carrying cuts of fresh meat.

Oh, and Jehanne made eyes at André Le Blanc all afternoon. Let her!

Le 12 juillet 1755

I am so tired I could sleep standing up! We spent the day salting down the rest of the meat to keep it from spoiling. Mémère says she will relish a taste of salt beef tongue. She is welcome to it!

Le 13 juillet 1755

With all the excitement and work these last days we have had little time to talk about Papa. Of course we worry about him all the time underneath. And about our dear Victor, too. We still have no news of him. I miss his jokes. And I never thought I would miss his teasing, but I do.

I have been scratching some little red spots around my ankles. I suppose Griffon has picked up fleas somewhere.

Le 15 juillet 1755

Papa is a prisoner! Oncle Paul got the bad news from some men of Pigiguit. The governor greeted Papa and the others in a rage. He demanded that they at once swear an oath promising to take up arms against the French if they are asked to do so. Of course our elders said no. Papa has always said that Acadians are neutrals. That means we do not fight either the French or the English. Well, except for some rebels like Beausoleil Broussard and our Victor. But the French are our kinfolk. How could we ever fight against them? When our elders said that to Governor Lawrence, he clapped them in jail. Now he wants new delegates chosen, and they, too, must go to Halifax. Will he put *them* in jail, if they do not do what he wants? And what will he do after that?

Maman says we can only wait and pray. Well, I am going to pray to *le bon Dieu* to send a plague upon that wicked governor!

Le 16 juillet 1755

Something woke me last night. A smothered sound. Maman was weeping, and I heard her moan Papa's name over and over again. I lay awake, sorrowing, not knowing how to comfort her. I suppose she grieves the more because she was so cross with Papa. *Hélas*, I know only too well what it feels like to repent too-hasty words and deeds.

I have just had an odd thought. Perhaps I get

my temper from Maman. I had not thought I was the least bit like her!

Le 17 juillet 1755

I am in disgrace again, and my heart is sore. Yesterday Maman sent me on an errand *chez* Oncle Paul. Of course, Geneviève and I fell to talking about what happened in Halifax. And Geneviève said she was glad *her* papa was wise enough not to sign the petition and so had kept out of trouble. I was furious. She meant *my* papa was not wise! Well, Geneviève has long curls and before I thought, I grabbed a handful and gave them a good yank. She burst into tears and so did I. I cried all the way home. Maman, of course, soon got out of me what I had done. I told her Geneviève deserved what she got for being mean about Papa, but Maman says I must go and apologize. I will not. So I am writing this up in the *grenier*, where she has sent me to think it over. I have had to miss my dinner and am very hungry, even though Belle slipped up with a slice of bread and lard.

Plus tard:

It is very late, but I cannot sleep before I write this. I gave in. I had to — I could not bear how bad I was feeling. Oh, how I wish I would learn to keep my temper like Catherine and Belle! And I felt guilty for grieving Maman when we have so many troubles. Especially as Papa told me to be good to her. So after the evening milking I told her I would apologize. She told me to make haste, and to be home before dark.

So back I went to Oncle Paul's. Griffon trotted ahead. He kept looking back as if to ask why I walked so slowly. But Geneviève came out at once when I asked for her, and the moment we saw each other we both burst into tears and fell into each other's arms. I apologized and she apologized, too, and suddenly my heart felt light as dandelion fluff. Geneviève confessed her maman had found her out, too, and said she deserved a switching for having spoken unkindly about Papa.

I had supper *chez* Oncle Paul and Tante Cécile, and the sun was going down as I walked home. Rosy light washed the sky and reflected in the bay, and the blue Cobeguit hills seemed to float in a pearly mist. I felt so happy and so at peace that I said a little prayer to *le bon Dieu*, thanking him for letting us live in our beautiful country and among our dear kin.

Le 18 juillet 1755

Catherine came today to help us with jam making. As I was kicking off my *sabots* outside the door, I overheard Maman telling her all about me and Geneviève. Catherine laughed and said it was high time someone taught Geneviève to mind her tongue — and Maman agreed! Yet yesterday she made me believe what I did was a terrible sin. Now I do not know what to think! Why do grown-ups tell you one thing when they really think something different? It is a puzzle.

Le 20 juillet 1755

Something amazing has happened! This evening I looked up from my milking to find a strange man standing in the barn door. My heart leaped into my throat, for he looked like a pirate, with a bushy beard and long shaggy hair. And he had a musket!

He grinned, and asked if I did not know him. And then by his voice I did. It was Victor! I shouted his name, but he shushed me. Then he told me to fetch Papa. So I had to tell him about Halifax, and what had happened to Papa and the others. A savage look of anger passed over his face, and he swore that *les maudits Anglais* would pay for what they had done.

I ran for Maman. When I told her Victor was in the stable, she turned salt white and dropped a bowl with a crash, then ran out to see him. I was full of joy that Victor was back.

He told Maman he cannot stay. He has come only to make sure we are well, and to gather news for Beausoleil. Maman pleaded with him to give up fighting *les Anglais*, but he said that he would never abandon Beausoleil. He warned her that Grand-Pré is full of wagging tongues, and that if word got out that he was back, there would soon be redcoats at the door to cart him off to prison like Papa.

He would stay only long enough to eat supper. I took it out to him in the barn, for he would not come into the house because the little ones might tell about seeing him. The only one Maman told was Claude. He went out to try to change Victor's mind, but it was no use.

"*Adieu, p'tite soeur*," Victor said, when I went to get his empty plate. He begged me to tell Papa when he came home how much he loved him. Then he hugged me and slipped away through the orchard. He — Oh, but I have only just this minute realized something. Victor said *adieu*, not *au revoir*. He was saying goodbye forever!

Le 22 juillet 1755

Two hundred and three men of our area have signed a new petition to Governor Lawrence. They will not agree to fight against the French, but promise to stay neutral, as always. We are all very proud of them, but very frightened, too. I cannot help wishing that Papa and all these others were not quite so brave.

Now I sound like Maman!

Le 24 juillet 1755

More of the most respected men of our village have been chosen to carry the petition to the governor. This time Oncle Paul went. Geneviève cried and cried, and I did not know how to comfort her. What will *les Anglais* do to them? How many more of our people will vanish into their prisons?

Le 26 juillet 1755

There is news from Port-Royal! Oncle Pierre says a rider came through today. The British have been defeated in a big battle at Fort Duquesne in the west of the colony of Penn-something. (I could not quite hear the word Oncle Pierre said to

Maman — it is a very odd name.)

Well, it serves the British right! Now *they* know how it feels to be on the losing side. But Oncle Pierre thinks *les Anglais* will be very angry at all French people now, and may make us Acadians suffer for it. I think *les Anglais* have been nasty enough already, *moi*. At least, Governor Lawrence has!

Le 28 juillet 1755

At Mass yesterday, our good Père Chauvreulx said special prayers for all our men in Halifax. Everyone wept, for every family has some relative in the hands of *les Anglais*. Surely *le bon Dieu* will protect Papa and the rest, and set them free!

Le 29 juillet 1755

Tomorrow we must begin the hay harvest while the weather continues fine. It cannot wait, for just one heavy rain could spoil the whole crop. Other folk do not have this burden. But Papa always grows sweet hay for his horses. Salt hay from the marsh is well enough for the cows and sheep, but not for his precious Perle! I cannot begrudge the task, as it is for Papa. But it will be hard, hard labour with our hearts so heavy. And without Papa and Victor, Maman and I must help Claude and Zachary. Mémère and Belle will see to the house and the cooking between them. And Belle will do most of the milking, for we will stay late in the fields. Belle is good at milking, for she is patient and gentle. The cows like her touch and let down their milk for her. Sometimes they hold it back from me when I am out of temper. I wonder how they know.

Le 30 juillet 1755

Too tired from haying to write more than this!

Le 31 juillet 1755

André Le Blanc and his older brother came to help us with the haying. I told André that I was never so pleased to see anyone in my life, and he blushed. Then I blushed. Why do I never think before I speak?

With more help, the hay fairly flies into the rick. Some is so dry that we piled it into the cart to go to the hayloft right away. The rest we stacked to dry. Maman praised André for being such a hard worker, and really, I like him so much better now that he is not showing off. Of course Jehanne is still welcome to flirt with him if she likes. *Some* boys might like a bold-faced wench like her!

Le 1er août 1755

My arms are so stiff from cutting hay that I can hardly write, and my back is one big ache. I can only drag myself around, groaning. But Maman is amazing. She swings her sickle hour after hour, with only the shortest break for a sip of barley water now and then. When I asked her how she could be so strong, she smiled, and there was a look in her eyes as if she was remembering something wonderful. She said that when she and Papa were first married, they had to build up the farm, and do all the work themselves. She said that though it was hard, it was a good time, too. Then tears sprang into her eyes, and she turned away. I knew she was thinking of Papa in prison in Halifax. Oh, when will we see him again? And how can I complain about my aches and pains when our dear Papa is a prisoner?

Le 2 août 1755

The only good thing about haying is that it makes you too tired to worry. I can hardly keep my eyes open to write this. Today was fair and hot like yesterday. Perfect for the hay, but hard for the hay makers labouring under the blazing sun.

But I want to write about the odd thing that happened. About mid aftenoon, a tiny cloud appeared out of nowhere in the eastern sky and built and built into a towering mass of white and grey. People called to each other and pointed as it drifted toward us, for it was very like a great angel with wings outspread. We felt the cool breath of its shadow on our faces as it passed over us, and a little breeze sprang up and raced through the fields with a sound like a sigh. Then the cloud moved slowly over Cap Baptiste and out to sea, and in a few moments it had vanished. The returning sun was hot, yet I shivered and my heart felt strangely heavy. It still does.

Le 3 août 1755

I cannot believe it, though I saw it happen with my own eyes! *Les Anglais* have taken our dear Père Chauvreulx! Soldiers stormed by on the main road as we were walking to church. People ran after them, expecting another proclamation. But when we got to the church we saw the soldiers had seized our priest. There was an angry roar from the crowd, but Père Chauvreulx bade us be calm. He told us to take away the sacred vessels from the church, put a covering on the altar and set the big crucifix there. He promised that the Lord will be our priest now. Then he lifted his hand and blessed us, making the sign of the cross. The soldiers put him astride a horse and tied his feet to the stirrups and his hands to the pommel of the saddle. Then they rode away with him. Jeremy was among them, and he looked ashamed. He is not a monster like the others.

When the soldiers were gone, we bowed our heads and prayed that *les Anglais* would not harm Père Chauvreulx. He has never done anything but good among us, and has always told us to be loyal subjects of the British. And this is how they treat him! He is a dear, kind man. I have loved him ever since he was so patient when I made mistakes saying my catechism. He was never cross at all. How dare they drag him away! May God punish them for it!

Le 5 août 1755

Losing Père Chauvreulx is a heavy blow. No one talks of anything else. How can we bear our troubles without the comfort of going to Mass? And how will people get married or buried or baptize their babies? Do the British expect us to live like animals?

People whisper that the angel-shaped cloud was an omen that foretold this sorrow and other evils to come.

Le 7 août 1755

The good thing about a farm is that you cannot neglect things. You have to keep busy every single moment. The bad thing about a farm is the very same! We only stop working to fall into our beds at night. Sleep comes easily, but I have uneasy dreams that I cannot quite remember in the morning.

Le 9 août 1755

The weather has continued hot and dry. The wheat stands tall in the fields, its heavy heads waving in the salt breeze. Soon it, too, will have to be harvested. Just the thought makes me groan. We have always worked hard, but nothing compared to this!

Le 11 août 1755

I said to Maman that perhaps Catherine could come to help us out in the fields when we begin to harvest the wheat. She shook her head and said that Catherine has enough work of her own to do these days. And that she must not do such heavy labour just now.

I thought Catherine must be ill, but when I asked, Maman said she was in perfect health. She and Mémère exchanged glances, and both were smiling. Another puzzle.

Le 13 août 1755

Zachary went roaming around up on the barrens below the South Mountain and came home very blue about the mouth. He says he found the biggest crop of blueberries he has ever seen. That means a kind of holiday for Belle and me tomorrow, for we must get to the blueberries before the bears do.

Le 14 août 1755

Belle and I and *les cousines* took our baskets up to the barrens. Maman made us take *les Terreurs*, too. Much help *they* were! Probably Maman just wanted some peace and quiet for herself for once. We picked and picked and picked. Marie-Josèphe at least tried to help, though she kept spilling her basket of berries and ours too. But Josèph-Marie kept wandering off. I warned him to keep near, but then I turned my back on him for no more than a moment and he vanished. We all rushed around calling his name, but he did not answer. To make matters worse, Marie-Josèphe threw herself down and began to howl. It takes more patience to deal with twins than I will *ever* have!

Just when I had decided we must run home and fetch help to find Josèph-Marie, he came running out of the woods yelling that a bear was after him! *Les cousines* screamed, and Marie-Josèphe wailed louder than ever. But I could see nothing, and Griffon did not bark. Besides, with the noise we were making, any sensible bear would have run a league by now.

I seized Josèph-Marie by his shirt collar and demanded whether he had really seen a bear. He nodded, opening his eyes wide and looking *très innocent*. But *moi,* I think the little rascal made the whole thing up.

Luckily, we had enough berries to fill our baskets, so home we went. Josèph-Marie capered ahead of us all the way.

Le 15 août 1755

Jam making again. The house smells sweet, but oh, it is hot! *Les Terreurs'* faces are purple from eating the sticky scum we skim off the boiling pots of fruit and sugar.

Blueberry jam was ever Papa's favourite. I poured some into an earthenware jar and labelled it with his name. If anyone else dares to touch it they will hear from Angélique Richard!

Le 16 août 1755

Belle and *les cousines* have gone back to the barrens for more berries, but I had to stay home to help Maman boil up the ones we have. It is late afternoon now, and I am limp with heat. I have come up to the orchard to cool off and write this. Zachary has gone to swim in the river, and I wish I could do the same. Boys always have more fun!

Le 18 août 1755

Yesterday I saw three pretty ships. I cannot remember seeing so many at once before. This morning I ran up to look for them, but they were gone. I wonder why they came?

Today Maman and I will spread out the blueberries Belle and the others picked yesterday. Drying them in the sun is not as hot work as boiling them into jam! And they will still make good pies during the winter. I will have to keep a close eye on Griffon, though. He loves to eat blueberries!

Plus tard:

The ships came back, and this time it looks as though they will stay. They anchored in the mouth of the Rivière Gaspereau, and boats full of soldiers came ashore! Zachary was down to the river and says the men are drawn up in ranks on the shore. They have blue coats, not like the red coats of the troops from Fort Edward. Claude says that means they are New Englanders, not English. *C'est curieux.* What are New England troops doing here? The commander of the soldiers is named Colonel Winslow. We know because he has posted proclamations summoning all the elders and other important people to meet with him tomorrow morning at nine o'clock in the church. At least the proclamations were in French this time.

Le 19 août 1755

Colonel Winslow told our elders that he has come to take charge of Grand-Pré. At least they think that is what he said, for Oncle Pierre said he spoke in English and the elders did not understand all of it. He did make them understand that he is short of provisions, though. We will have to sell him food until his supply ships arrive. Claude says one good thing about the New Englanders is that they pay in real coins, not just the paper money like the garrison at Annapolis Royal. Oncle Pierre thinks the troops are here to rebuild the old fort. He says now they have kicked the French out of Fort Beauséjour, they mean to keep their eyes on us. Maman shakes her head, and says that soldiers always bring trouble.

Le 21 août 1755

C'est un scandale! The soldiers are storing weapons in our church. And they have started building a wooden palisade around the church-yard. Why do they not use the old fort and leave our church alone?

Le 22 août 1755

Soldiers or no soldiers, the wheat must be harvested. We begin on Monday.

Plus tard:

I am very frightened, for Jeremy Witherspoon has told me a secret. He came from Fort Edward with a message to Colonel Winslow and stopped off at our farm on his way back. *Grâce à Dieu* I was alone in the house when he came.

Jeremy says that something dreadful is going to happen to all the Acadians of Grand-Pré. Colonel Winslow and Colonel Murray at Fort Edward are plotting it, sending messengers back and forth all the time. All the soldiers are sworn to secrecy, and if anyone finds out Jeremy has talked to me he will be flogged!

Jeremy says our family must run away — just leave everything and slip off to the woods without telling anyone! But he would not say why, because to tell would break his soldier's oath. He has gone now, leaving me to fret about what he told me. I should tell Maman and Claude, but then I will have to confess about knowing Jeremy. And that will get me into great trouble, *pour sûr*. What am I going to do?

Le 23 août 1755

I had to tell, of course. *Hélas*, I was surely right about getting into trouble. Maman is very angry with me. She says I am a disgrace to the family. I pleaded that Jeremy is my friend and that he is only trying to help us.

Maman called me *une petite idiote*, yet in the end she heard me out. She can be hard, but she is fair. She said Jeremy *might* be telling the truth, because he lives with the soldiers and would know about the danger. But Claude said we ought not to trust him because he would not say what the danger was. Besides, if we run away now we will lose our harvest. And the British would take our land, *pour sûr*.

Maman is even more worried about what might happen to Papa in Halifax. They might punish him if we ran off. And how could we go without warning all our kinfolk, too? So she and Claude decided to wait until we know more. She told me to go to bed and tell no one else what Jeremy said.

And so I crept away to write this.

Le 24 août 1755

This is the third Sunday since *les Anglais* took away our good Père Chauvreulx. How we miss him! We miss the glad sound of the church bells, too, that used to turn our thoughts toward Heaven. We cannot even go into our church to say a prayer, for it is full of horrible weapons. Of course Maman gathers us around her for Sunday prayers, but it is not the same. We see nobody now except our closest neighbours, for there is nowhere to meet and share news. I miss gossiping outside the church. It is as if all Grand-Pré is holding its breath, waiting, waiting. But for what?

Le 25 août 1755

Today we begin the harvest. The three of us seem so few on our great field. Our hay crop was small compared to this! But somehow we must bring in the grain. Across the boundary ditches, *les* Melanson were already at their work as we bent to ours. Stoop, seize a fistful of wheat, cut it with a sweep of the sickle, spread it in swathes to dry. Stoop, cut, spread, on and on and on. Then when the grain has dried enough, pile it into sheaves, all the while under the fierce sun. Maman and I wore our broad-brimmed caps, but still our faces and arms were burned by the sun. Belle and Zachary brought our dinner in hampers so we need not trek up to the house. I wolfed my share down, splashed water on my hot face, and then it was time to start in again. Only with the blessed, blessed dusk did we stop work and trudge home for supper. I am half asleep writing this.

Le 26 août 1755

This afternoon Basile and André Le Blanc and others arrived to help us. Their fathers have spared them to us, though every family needs every pair of hands available. May God bless them!

It is amazing how well I like André now that I have got to know him better. As we ate our dinner, I gave him just the tiniest hint about Jehanne, and he looked puzzled. He has not even noticed her flirting. It serves her right!

Le 27 août 1755

I *try* to think about other things, but my thoughts always creep back to what Jeremy said. I do not think he would risk being found out, to tell me something false. One thing is certain, the soldiers are here to stay. Every day they build their palisade higher, and we hear their drums and trumpets at all hours. The palisade keeps us out, but not them in. Madame Hébert told Madame Le Blanc and she told Tante Cécile that the soldiers steal things from the farms round about. May *le bon Dieu* protect us!

Le 30 août 1755

Three more ships in the bay. Big ones. Our men mutter among themselves and stare at them. What do *les Anglais* need so many ships for? They do not unload anything.

Le 1ᵉʳ septembre 1755

Now Basile drives the *charrette*. That was always Victor's job. He and Claude pile the heavy golden sheaves into the *charrette* and our patient oxen pull it up to the barn. Maman and André and I work in a line, backs bent like bows, stooping and cutting. André is a hard worker, almost as good as Claude. He seems at ease with us now, and often has a joke to tell. It makes the work go faster. Griffon greets him, tail wagging, whenever he comes, and that shows that he is truly a good person. Whyever did I fancy that I disliked him?

Le 2 septembre 1755

Oncle Pierre came across to our field late this afternoon, and we all gathered around. Colonel

Winslow has issued another proclamation. All the men and all boys over the age of ten are to go to the church on Friday at three in the afternoon to hear a message. As if we have time for such nonsense in the middle of the harvest! But Oncle Pierre says they will have to go, or Colonel Winslow will send soldiers to take away everything we have. He does not seem worried, though, and says it must only be about our selling more provisions to the troops. Though he grumbles that as yet they have paid us nothing for what we have already given them.

But *I* worry. Why do they need boys as young as ten to talk about provisions? Does Oncle Pierre not think it strange?

Le 3 septembre 1755

It was cool again last night. Summer has gone. After another long day in the fields, we returned this evening to find poor Belle sound asleep at the table with her head pillowed on her arms. Mémère had let her sleep a while as she was so weary. Yet our supper was ready and waiting. I cannot help complaining about having to do such heavy work. But Belle cooks and milks and tends the poultry and the garden. Just keeping *les Terreurs* out of trouble is task enough!

Le 4 septembre 1755

Still another ship has come into the bay. With each one, our hearts grow heavier. Sailors come ashore from them and make trouble like the soldiers. These New Englanders seem to hate us worse than *les Anglais* have ever done. Claude says it is because French troops and Indians are fighting them in the West, so they blame us for it. As if the King of France asks *us* about who he fights!

Le 5 septembre 1755

It is too terrible . . . I still cannot believe . . . I have wept until I can weep no more. But that changes nothing. My dear brothers . . . they are prisoners! Colonel Winslow has locked all our young men up. We know not if he will let them out again. And if Jeremy is right, there will be worse to come — far worse!

Claude and Zachary went off with the rest after dinner to meet with Colonel Winslow at the church. It breaks my heart now to think how proud Zachary was to be among the menfolk. He is just ten. He was whistling as he capered off at Claude's side. Without the boys there was not much we could do in the fields, so Maman told me to help Belle. But I disobeyed. I was burning to see Colonel Winslow for myself and hear the news. So I slipped off after Claude and Zachary.

I got to the church in time to see them file inside the palisade with the others. Soldiers prodded people along with their muskets. It seemed to me that no one was in much of a hurry to see the high and mighty colonel. I tried to slip inside, too, but a soldier pushed me back. I decided to wait till they came out. That way I would hear their news first.

When all were inside the church, the guards closed the doors and set a great bar across them This puzzled me much — why would they lock up our menfolk when all had come freely? Then I heard someone calling my name. It was Jeremy.

I asked why our menfolk were locked inside the church. Jeremy said — it is horrible, I still cannot believe it! — that we are to be deported. I did not understand the word, but Jeremy explained. It means *les Anglais* are going to send all Acadians south to the British colonies. Our land is forfeit. Everything belongs to the British now and our harvest will go to feed others!

They are only waiting for enough ships to arrive, before they send us away. Meanwhile, our menfolk are hostages.

I called Jeremy a liar and a *maudit Anglais*, and ran home weeping. He must be lying. He *must*! Acadia belongs only to the Acadians. The British have no right to it! But when I said this to Maman, she shook her head. She said that in this world people with great power do whatever they want.

But why does *le bon Dieu* let them? *Why?*

Le 6 septembre 1755

Jeremy is not a liar after all, *hélas*. None of our men came back. This afternoon, Tante Cécile sent Geneviève over to find out if we had heard anything. Maman gently told her what we knew. Geneviève burst into tears, and we could hear her crying all the way back down the lane.

Ah, *les Anglais* are clever-cruel. Wives without husbands, mothers without sons, sisters without brothers, what can we do now but wait and pray? And still another ship has arrived. What a fool I was to find them beautiful and interesting at first! And I remember what Jeremy said. Will this one make enough ships for the British to carry out their wicked plan? I have never liked *les Anglais*, but now I *hate* them!

Plus tard:

Mémère says that hate is a sin, no matter what. But how can I help it?

Le 7 septembre 1755

Zachary came home but he could not stay. It is only that *les Anglais* have sent some of the younger ones home to help with the harvest. But they all have to go back tonight, or the rest of the prisoners will be punished. Of course it is Sunday, and we do no work in the fields. *Les Anglais* did not think of that! And our men surely did not remind them! Why would they miss a chance for some of them to go home?

Maman wanted to know what else Colonel Winslow had said. Zachary told us that he read a long proclamation he could not understand, but that Claude said it meant we would all be sent far away on ships. Then Zachary asked if *les Anglais* could really do that.

If they had human hearts instead of stones in their chests they could not. How can Acadians live anywhere except Acadia?

We cannot finish the harvest. Zachary is too small to manage the oxen, and Maman and I are not strong enough to lift the sheaves of wheat onto the *charrette*. What are we going to do? If the grain stays in the fields it will be spoiled, and then *les Anglais* will punish us!

We have prepared food for Claude and Zachary. Colonel Winslow has ordered the families of the prisoners to feed them. He would not dream of wasting his precious supplies on Acadians!

Le 8 septembre 1755

Today it was Claude's turn to come. He says he managed to make the British understand that the little boys would not be enough help to get in the harvest. And the British want our grain for themselves! So Colonel Winslow agreed that older prisoners could take turns going home.

It is horrible to have to work ourselves to death to feed *les Anglais*. But Claude says that if we do not, the soldiers will take all we have at gunpoint and leave us to starve. Something has changed in Claude. He has ever been gentle and peaceful. Now he is full of hate. I know too well how he feels. But — it is hard even to find words for this — seeing his face so hard and his eyes so cold was like looking at a stranger. It frightens me. I am afraid of my own hate now. I will pray not to feel it.

Maman says that we must hope that *les Anglais* will change their minds, that surely *le bon Dieu* will not let them send us away.

So we spent another long day in the fields. And the harder we work, the more will go to feed the wicked enemies who seek to destroy us!

Le 9 septembre 1755

I went down to the church today with a hamper of food for Claude and Zachary. The guards let us womenfolk into the churchyard, but Claude was not there. So I looked for him inside the church. It smells of unwashed bodies. Small wonder! More than three hundred men and boys are cooped up there at night. Claude was with a knot of other young men. He took the basket and shooed me away. He said it was not good for me to be near the guards.

On my way out, I came upon an officer standing before the house of Père Chauvreulx. It must have been Colonel Winslow himself, for we have heard that he lives there now. I took a good hard look at him. He is a plump fellow, with a round rosy face and a double chin above his gold-crusted collar. Under his officer's hat he wears a strange white-powdered thing covering his hair.

He does not seem the kind of monster that would do such terrible things. Yet he looks pleased with himself. So he must be *very* wicked. I felt I should hate him for his cruelty to us. But I could not. It is very strange.

Le 10 septembre 1755

The British have

They have

Claude and Zachary are gone! Gone, without even a goodbye. Surely *le bon Dieu* will punish *les Anglais* for such cruelty. They have put all our young men aboard the ships. The soldiers said they were plotting an uprising. I hope they were! I wish it had succeeded! The British have no right to treat us like sheep they can drive as they wish.

If I had not gone down with provisions when I did, I would not even have caught a last glimpse of them. At the church I saw all our young men drawn up in rows on one side of the churchyard. Soldiers with muskets at the ready stood all around. And my foolish heart leaped with joy, for I thought they were setting our dear ones free.

But then an officer shouted orders, and I froze. Our menfolk were to march down to the shoreline. They would be put aboard the ships! Just the young ones. The older men must stay behind.

For a long moment no one spoke or moved. It was so still that I could hear the British flag on the church snapping in the wind. Then a boy cried out that he would not leave his father. At that, Colonel Winslow stepped forward. He seized the boy by the shoulder and shoved him hard, so that he stumbled forward. The soldiers fixed their bayonets and advanced upon the rest. An older boy stepped toward them. Scornfully, he tore open his shirt, baring his chest. He was daring them to kill him!

"Go, go my son! Do not lay down your life for my sake!" a voice called from the crowd of older men. At last the lines slowly moved forward. The smallest boys sobbed in terror, and the young men began to sing a hymn to comfort them. The men in the churchyard prayed out loud. I dropped to my knees in the dust, weeping. Soon more and more women came running, until the whole way to the harbour was lined with people crying and lamenting. I saw Claude and Zachary go by. Zachary's face was white with fear, but Claude's eyes were blazing. André passed, and for a moment his eyes clung to mine before a soldier prodded him forward.

I watched until the last of them were rowed out

to the ships. Then I ran home to tell Maman. She is desolate, and Mémere and Belle are weeping. Only the twins do not understand. My thoughts are hot with anger, but my heart is cold with dread. Will I ever see my dear brothers again in this world? Or will *les maudits Anglais* scatter the ships they are on to the four winds?

Le 11 septembre 1755

This morning I ran to the upper orchard to look down over the water. I feared some ships might have gone on the morning tide. But no. *Grâce à Dieu*, they are all there. I counted them over twice, just to be sure. So our dear ones are still with us! But for how long? What will *les Anglais* do to them? And to us, now that we are defenceless?

Le 12 septembre 1755

We move like dead creatures about the house and garden. There is so much work to do, yet we have not the heart for any of it. Oncle Pierre came this afternoon on his way back to the church. He said that Colonel Winslow brought in an orange-haired lad who spoke French to explain things to the prisoners. Jeremy! Oncle Pierre says we are to be allowed to carry provisions to the harbour for our people aboard the ships. At least we will know they are not starving.

Le 13 septembre 1755

Two ill-favoured soldiers in blue uniforms came today to see about the state of the harvest. Griffon is a good French dog and did not care for the look of them. He put up his hackles and showed his teeth, so I had to shut him in the barn. When the soldiers saw there was much still to be done, they tried to explain with gestures that their orders were to help us get the wheat crop in. I told them I understood English well enough. So we got the oxen hitched up and Maman and I trailed after them to the fields.

One soldier is not so bad. He says he is a farmer in New England, so at least he knows how things should be done. But he is hard-faced and tight-lipped and he likes us not. The other man is not much use at all. And his eyes rove all over our farmyard, as if he is gloating over what we have.

Le 14 septembre 1755

Most of our chickens are gone! There was a great clucking in the night, and I thought a fox had got among them. We had taken Griffon into the house, and he barked and barked, but Maman signed to me to quiet him. She had barred the door and pushed a heavy wooden chest across it. I wondered what she was afraid of, but in the morning I found out. The thieves were human, for there were boot prints everywhere. The villains broke down our fences and trampled the garden too. Not just the vegetables but even Maman's last marigolds are ground into the mud. How they must hate us! It makes me sick to see it.

Le 15 septembre 1755

Yesterday Maman took a basket to the shore, hoping to visit Claude and Zachary. But it was forbidden. The officer in charge of the longboat said that each family's basket goes to the right persons, but we cannot help wondering if that is true. It grieves us to think that Claude and Zachary may lack for something we could send them.

Le 16 septembre 1755

I slipped away this afternoon and went down to the river to visit the *Madeleine*. She is tied up at the dock and looks sad and neglected. There was water in her, so I bailed her out. Then I sat down and thought of Claude. Why do you only understand how important people are when they are gone? I love Victor and miss him. But losing Claude is worse. He has always been so good to me, taking my part even against Maman sometimes. And now he is troubled and I cannot help him. If he loses his kind, good nature it will be a terrible thing. But at least we know where he is. Not like Papa. *He* might die and we would never know!

I wept awhile sitting there in the *Madeleine*, with Griffon's heavy head on my lap. Then I dried my tears and we went home.

Le 17 septembre 1755

The weather has turned stormy, with much rain. The British ships did not send their longboats in to shore, though we waited and waited in the cold and wet. The prisoners will go hungry! We could hardly bear to eat our own dinner, knowing how empty their stomachs must be.

Le 18 septembre 1755

Another stormy day, and again, no boats. Every high tide we women cluster on the beach in the wind and rain with our laden baskets. But no boats come. Two days and no food for our men. I suppose the British have plenty of food aboard for their own sailors. They are cowardly and cruel not to send the boats!

Le 19 septembre 1755

I have had a frightening adventure, but *grâce à Dieu* I am alive to tell of it. There were no longboats again today. The gale was less, but the waves were high and rolling. I paced along the shore, gazing longingly at the ships. Then I came upon a rowboat drawn up on the strand. Somehow I got it into the water and pushed off. Soldiers ran after me, shouting, but I was too far out to be caught. I was sure I could reach the ship, but the waves kept crashing over the bow of the rowboat and soon it was half full of water. It was hard to row, and I began to be afraid. Then I heard a shout and saw a longboat from the ship bearing down on me. A wave broke over me, and there was a crash as the boats came together. I clung to my basket as someone dragged me aboard the longboat.

"What a brave lassie!" a voice said. An officer was smiling at me, and I wondered what a "lassie" was. He barked orders and the boat turned for the ship. And so the prisoners got a mouthful to eat today. Afterward, the officer brought me back safe to shore.

I had to explain to Maman why I was wringing wet, and then I got a sharp scolding for being foolhardy. Then she hugged me!

Le 20 septembre 1755

I have caught a bad cold. My throat is sore and my nose is plugged and I ache all over. Mémère dosed me with vile-tasting sulfur and molasses. I think her medicines are worse than my illness!

But I am still glad I did it!

Le 22 septembre 1755

The weather is fine, so Maman and Belle took the hamper to the beach. They carried clean clothing for Claude and Zachary. Belle was in tears when they came back. She cannot bear not knowing how things are for our brothers.

Le 23 septembre 1755

Still fine weather. This morning the blue line of the Cobeguit Hills stands out clear beyond the bay. But I can see thick columns of smoke coiling up. They say the British are burning Cobeguit village. They do it to strike fear into our hearts. Will it be the turn of Grand-Pré next?

Plus tard:

Rumours fly. We hear that there are French strangers over at Rivière Peraux urging folk to make a stand against the British. I hope they do! It is too late for us, with our menfolk prisoners. And the British know it!

If only the French would send an army to rescue us. But, *hélas*, they are far away in Canada and Louisbourg now. We are alone and helpless before our enemies. It is like a big cruel cat playing with a mouse!

Le 24 septembre 1755

Most people here still do not believe the worst will happen. But when I saw the smoke of Cobeguit, I felt as though a sliver of ice went through my heart. It is terrible to live like this, dreading the worst, but with everything around us looking *ordinaire*, as always.

Le 26 septembre 1755

Three more ships. How I hate to see them! They are like wolves gathering around a flock of sheep.

Le 30 septembre 1755

Yesterday evening a band of rough looking sol diers came. The bad one who came before to work on the harvest was their leader. The villain knew his way around. They went into the barn and started driving out the cattle. Griffon went wild barking, and I was afraid they might shoot him, so I ran out with a broom before Maman could stop me. I told them to leave our cows alone. The soldiers just smirked and said they had orders from Colonel Winslow to take them. Then they began driving the cattle down the lane. But Pâquerette was still inside the barn and I kept her back with the broom. One of the men growled at me, but another said to let me keep her.

Maman has forbidden me ever to argue with soldiers again, saying it is *trop dangereux*. I know she is right, and my knees shake now when I think on what I did. But I was just too angry to be careful!

Le 1ᵉʳ octobre 1755

I saw Jeremy when I went to take food to the ship. He looked very sad, and I repented calling him a *maudit Anglais*. After all, our trouble is not his fault, and he tried to help us. I told him so, and then I told him about the cows. He said he would report it. Colonel Winslow has forbidden his men to harm us. The soldiers who stole the chickens were found out and flogged. I do not understand how a man like Winslow can be fair and cruel at the same time.

Jeremy heard from one of the New England soldiers that Colonel Winslow keeps a diary and writes everything down. Of course, Jeremy does not know that I do, too. It seems strange, the two of us writing about what is happening. Colonel Winslow will not feel the same about it as I do, *pour sûr*! I think of him each time I write now. I do not want to, but I cannot help it.

May his wicked plans go awry! May he have to take his nasty soldiers out of our country!

Le 3 octobre 1755

Bad weather again. But still the longboats came, *grâce a Dieu*. I went to the shore, taking heavier clothing for Claude and Zachary. By the time they get it, everything will probably be soaked through. What use will it be in that damp ship?

Le 5 octobre 1755

People saw messengers on the main road from Halifax, and more on the road to Port-Royal. Maman sighed when she heard that, and said messengers mean more trouble. It is *horrible* to be helpless as we are, just waiting for our enemies to do what they will with us! Without our menfolk and their weapons we cannot defend ourselves. I feel as though I have a lump of lead inside me.

Le 7 octobre 1755

A day of rain and storm. We have sat indoors all day, fretting. Soldiers passed by yesterday and shouted that we must make ready to leave soon. Colonel Winslow will order us aboard the ships. Will they really do this cruel thing to us? I still cannot believe it. Surely

Plus tard:

I broke off because Geneviève ran in with news. Prisoners have escaped from the ships, twenty-four of them! Colonel Winslow has posted a list of names and says that if the men do not surrender, soldiers will hunt them down and shoot them. And Claude's name is on the list! When Maman heard that, she fainted dead away. Mémère and I have made her lie down. I am trying to stay calm, but my head is awhirl. Will they shoot Claude down like a wild animal?

And I have selfish thoughts, too. If they do send us away, what will we do without Claude? Oh, it is not like him to forget how much we need him. But I think I know where he will go to hide. He *must* come back or he will be killed. I will make him come!

Le 10 octobre 1755
Á bord du Leynord

Our dear familiar world is dead. It was killed by the British two days ago. Perhaps it would be kinder if they killed all of us too. We have been so terrified that all we could do is cling together and weep. We are still numb with fear. But I will try to write down what happened as best I can, though my hand trembles, and my tears blot the page.

It is three days since I set off to find Claude. I slipped away after supper on Tuesday, taking Griffon along for protection. I did not tell Maman where I was going, for I knew she would forbid me. I found Claude where I had guessed he would be, at a hunting shelter he and Victor built deep in the woods. Some of the others were with him. I told him it was his duty to come back, but he did not want to hear that. He only dreams of fighting the British now. Our gentle Claude — he has become so hard and angry!

He and the others were grateful for the provisions I brought, though. They all said it was too dangerous for me to go back, with bands of soldiers raiding the countryside. So I spent the night there in the woods with them, curled up against Griffon for warmth. In the morning, I set out for home alone, weeping.

When I got near the farm I could hear Pâquerette lowing and wondered that Belle had not milked her and turned her out to pasture. But then I saw that no smoke came from the chimney of our house. The door gaped wide open on its hinges, and the hearth was cold and dark. Many small things lay strewn about as if left behind in a hurry.

I screamed for Maman and Belle and Mémère, but there was no answer. They were gone.

For a moment I stood frozen with fear. Then I seized a sack lying on the floor and began throwing anything I could reach into it — this diary, my quilt bag, a loaf of bread, a candle, a cabbage . . . I ran to the barn and untied Pâquerette, and drove her and her calf down to the meadow. I opened the gate of La Gloire's sty too, and shooed the last few chickens out of their coop. Then I shouldered the sack and ran down the lane with Griffon on my heels. By Maman's willow, I stopped for one last look at our dear farm. Pulling out my pocket knife, I cut a willow slip and tucked it away. Then I ran along the road to Oncle Paul's. I hoped Maman and the others might be there, but Oncle Paul's house was deserted too, with the animals running wild in the barnyard. I ran on. Below the hill, I could see the mouth of the river all jammed with ships. Longboats scuttled like water beetles between them and the shore — longboats loaded with people!

A party of soldiers came tramping along. One pointed his musket at me and said I must hurry or be shot. I suppose he did not mean it, for the others laughed as I took to my heels. At last I caught up with a crowd moving slowly down to the beach. The road was choked with two-wheeled carts piled high with household goods. On some, ailing grandparents rode. Women, many carrying their babies, struggled to pull them along. Everyone, even the tiniest children, carried bundles on their backs. Babies wailed, and a low moan rose up from the people, the sound of weeping and praying.

I wormed my way through the crowd, stopping my ears when people begged my help. I felt wicked, but I had to find my family! At last I reached the shore, which was jammed with people and carts and baggage. As longboats came aground, soldiers forced people aboard them at musket point. They went, weeping, leaving most of their belongings behind. Worse, far worse, than the weeping was the screaming when those who were together were forced aboard different boats.

I swear I will never forget these sights, these sounds, until I am cold in my grave. My hand cramps and my heart is sick with sorrow. I can write no more.

Le 11 octobre

I must go on. Colonel Winslow, whose masters have set him to do this terrible deed, will be writing his account. I will write *mine*!

On the beach, there was no sign of my family. I saw familiar faces all around, yet they seemed the faces of strangers. How could I care for their sorrow when I had lost my loved ones? I saw Madame Granger, Louis's mother, sitting on a bundle. When I begged her for news of my family, she moaned that they were all gone away aboard the hungry waiting ships — she did not know which one. It was the same with all the other people I asked. Blank stares, a shake of the head.

At last I spied Jeremy helping an old woman into one of the boats. Sobbing, I seized him by the lapels and begged him to help me. He said everything was confused, that no one really knew which family was on which ship, and that the ships would go to different ports. If I did not find the right ship, I would never see my family again!

We rushed up and down the beach, questioning the crew of each returning longboat. At least Jeremy's red coat got their attention. But it was no use. They could not remember my family among so many. At last I fell on my knees in the sand, weeping, while Griffon tried to lick my tears away. But Jeremy dragged me up. At the farthest end of the strand, another longboat was loading, and we hurried to it. I recognized the officer in charge. He was the one who had rescued me from drowning.

He remembered me too. But his eyes were sad and he said that this time he could not save me. Jeremy explained how I had lost my family, and the officer asked if there was anything special about them that he might remember. I knew not what to say. To me they were the dearest folk in the world. Yet what would a stranger see but another weary woman with children and an aged mother? Suddenly I thought of Belle. Surely an angel of Heaven made me think of her. I cried that my sister was very fair, with the biggest bluest eyes anyone had ever seen.

The officer's face lit up, and he said he had seen a girl with eyes like the bluebells of Scotland not an hour before. She got into a longboat beside his, that belonged to the *Leynord*.

Jeremy and I sped back down the shore, demanding the ship's name of every longboat. At last we found one for the *Leynord*. It was almost full, but I shoved my way aboard. Griffon tried to follow me, but the sailors pushed him back.

As the boat pulled away, I was stricken with fear. What if my family were not aboard the *Leynord*? I would be lost and alone forever! For one wild moment I wanted to leap into the sea and swim for shore. But I huddled down and whispered a prayer to *le bon Dieu*.

Suddenly a seaman fired his musket at something in the water. I saw the wet head of some animal swimming after us. It was Griffon! The shot hit near him, but he swam on. Bracing myself in the rocking boat, I stood up and pointed toward shore. "*En arrière*, Griffon!" I shouted. I had sent him to the back of the pasture for the cows a thousand times with that command. He always obeyed, and did so this last time. His dear, faithful head turned back. I saw him come safe out of the water, and Jeremy ran to meet him. But my heart was aching. Then I thought that perhaps the army would not let Jeremy keep a dog, that the soldiers might still shoot Griffon! But I could only trust in *le bon Dieu*. Surely in His mercy He will not let my good dog suffer. Through my tears I watched and watched until Jeremy's red coat was only a dot on the distant shore.

At last the wooden belly of the ship loomed over us. One after another we climbed a rope ladder. A seaman hauled me over the railing, and I screamed the name *Richard* in his ear. He just shook his head and shoved me onward. My heart filled with despair. Then a voice cried my name, and someone threw herself on me. It was Belle!

I have finished. My dear ones are all here with me in this dark place. We are crowded in like sheep in a fold, but *grâce à Dieu* we are together.

Le 12 octobre 1755

I said all my dear ones are here, but it is not so. Claude and Zachary are not with us, and Papa, of course. And the Le Blancs were sent aboard a different ship, so poor Catherine had to choose which family to go with. Bollo says she wept and wept, but in the end she went with Basile's family, hoping against hope that the British will put Basile on the same ship. Maman's eyes are swollen with much weeping. Belle whispered to me that it is not just about Catherine but also for her baby that is coming. I feel so foolish! Belle guessed the secret all along, but I just thought Catherine was getting fat! Now I know what those wise looks between Maman and Mémère were about.

We Acadians are one big family. It is *trop cruel* to tear us apart like this! We have lost our uncles and aunts and *les cousines*, too. *Ma pauvre* Geneviève! Will I ever see you again? And André — now that we have become friends I miss him, too. And Belle grieves for Marie-Blanche and Marie-Madeleine. We have only each other now.

Le 13 octobre 1755

I fear for our dear Mémère. She does not speak nor will she eat. She just smiles and smiles and looks right through us. Maman shakes her head. Mémère's mind has always been *très clair* despite all her aches and pains. But now it is as if a veil has come down behind her eyes. I do not think she even knows us now, or where she is. One of the women told Maman that perhaps that is God's mercy. But how can it be a mercy to lose your mind?

Le 14 octobre 1755

The days drag. We have always been so busy, with never a moment to spare. Now there is nothing to do but wait. You would think that fear and sorrow would make folk kinder, but it is not so. People snap at each other over the least thing, and grumble that others have more than they do, even in this wretched place. Half a loaf of bread more for one family brings black looks and bitter words. It does not help to have *les* Melanson aboard, because of Jehanne. She is so bossy — already she has made herself the leader of the other girls here. I wish *les Anglais* had put her on another ship!

The crowding is what makes everything so bad, for we cannot escape each other. We live like moles in the dark in this wooden room without windows. It is too low for any but the shortest among us to stand upright, and too crowded for all of us to lie down at once. There are hogsheads full of water, but they must last the whole journey. So we are allowed to take only a little each day to drink. Our meals are cooked inside a strange wooden structure up on deck. There is an iron stove where they boil up beef with cabbage or turnips. Besides that we get bread and sometimes apples to eat. Of course people brought what provisions they could, but so much had to be left behind.

Le 16 octobre 1755

I have found myself the tiniest corner behind a curved rib of the ship where I can curl up with my back bent and write for a while. A little light falls down from the hatchway, which is left open unless it rains. But it is hard to write here. There is so much noise, and some give me hard looks, as if I am doing something wrong. Certainly Jehanne does. I heard her telling the other girls that I give myself airs just because I can read and write.

Well, I *am* proud of that, it is true. Belle says to pay no attention to Jehanne. That is easy to say, but not so easy to do. People like Jehanne have a way of making themselves noticed!

With my pocket knife I notch the ship's rib to mark the passing days.

Le 18 octobre 1755

They let us up on deck a handful at a time for an hour each day. I live for a breath of fresh air and the chance to stretch and walk about. Sometimes I feel I will suffocate down here in the dark. But it rains and rains, and our cloaks get soaked through. The hold smells of wet wool. Today is no different. The sea and the sky are grey alike, and I could not see the beloved shore. But I smelled smoke. Folk say *les Anglais* are burning our farms! I pray it is not true.

Le 20 octobre 1755

A boat came alongside today. We heard a thump as it hit the side of the *Leynord*, then the tramp of feet across the deck over our heads. Then legs came down the hatchway — men's legs. And the second pair that came down was Zachary's! Belle and I trampled people to get to him. He looked very frightened at first, then when he saw us he burst into tears. Our uncles have looked after him since Claude escaped, but then the British took them away to other ships and he feared he would be left alone or put on a ship with strangers. But, *grâce à Dieu*, after two days they brought him here.

Zachary is much changed now. He seems quieter and makes no mischief. How I would have welcomed that once! Now I miss his tricks.

Lucky Jehanne! She got her brother *and* her papa back today.

Le 22 octobre 1755

Belle takes Marie-Josèphe and I take Josèph-Marie and we try to keep them quiet with games and stories so that Maman can watch over Mémère. She still eats no more than a spoonful of broth. Maman talks to her all the time in a low voice, asking her this and that and reminding her of all the things that need to be done before winter. Of course we cannot do any of them now. I think Maman is trying to talk Mémère back to us from wherever she has gone in her mind. But it seems to do no good, and tires Maman much. I pray every night for Mémère to get better.

Le 23 octobre 1755

Mémère was restless in the night and I got up to soothe her before Maman woke. She *must* sleep. The rain had stopped and the hatch was open to let in some air. I gazed up through it at the moon, which was clear and bright. I almost wept to see its familiar face. I cannot believe I will never see it rise over our orchard again.

To pass the time today I counted how many of us are in the hold of the *Leynord*. There are one hundred and seventy-eight of us, now that the men have returned. All of us know each other, of course, for Grand-Pré is such a small place. But Papa's brothers and sisters and their families are not here. Nor are other neighbours, *les* Le Blanc and *les* Hébert. *Les* Melanson we have one too many of, say I, and her name begins with *J*!

Le 24 octobre 1755

Maman is worn to a shadow of herself with watching over Mémère. She tries to do too much, and will not let Belle and me help her. She says that we must not worry, that she needs to be doing something.

We all do. Maman and Belle were wise enough to tuck their knitting into their bundles. So they keep useful and busy. Of course I never thought of such a thing. Belle has offered to share her knitting with me, but she will be sorry when she sees my uneven stitches!

I have been thinking how I used to hate chores. Now I miss them. Will someone milk Pâquerette and look after her? Or is she running wild in the woods? And Griffon — oh, I cannot bear to think of Griffon!

Plus tard:

Jehanne came over to visit with us. I do not know why she bothered, as she has nothing pleasant to say. But I suppose "sticking pins" in people gives her something to do. Belle was brushing her hair to keep it shiny, and Jehanne said it was wicked to be so vain in the midst of our great trouble. I told her that if her hair were as silky as Belle's, perhaps she would brush it more often and look the better for it. She took herself off in a fit of spite. Maman shook her head at me and said I must try to be kinder, and Belle said I need not have quarrelled with Jehanne on her account. But who would not stand up for her own sister?

Le 25 octobre 1755

Why, oh why, did the British put us all aboard ships only to leave us here? Perhaps they do not mean to send us away at all, and will just keep us here until we die. The thought frightens me. Even worse is to wonder what will happen to our family if they do send us away. Others have their husbands and grown-up brothers now, but not we Richards. How will we live, just women and children as we are? Will we starve to death in a foreign land among strangers? *Le bon Dieu* must mean to punish us. But what have we done to deserve it?

Le 26 octobre 1755

It is like a miracle. They have brought Claude to us. And we had been sure we would never see him again! How wicked I was to doubt *la bonté de Dieu*! Claude gave me a hug that nearly cracked my ribs when he saw me. He calls me his conscience, and told Maman how I nagged him to give himself up. He says no sooner had he sent me off home than he knew in his heart that I was right.

The British did not punish him when he gave himself up. Most of the others who escaped did the same, so they could go on the ships with their families. But two others were shot trying to hide in the woods.

The best thing of all is that Claude is his old self again. I do not know why, but somehow he has left his hatred behind him. Even when he saw how we live here, how ill Mémère is, he did no more than cross himself. He says he will leave revenge in the hands of *le bon Dieu*. It is such a comfort to have him whole again.

Le 27 octobre 1755

We have put out to sea! There was a huge bustle on deck this morning. Sailors shouted orders and footsteps thumped overhead. Claude raised his head, listening, and said that they were weighing anchor. Suddenly the ship seemed to come alive under our feet.

There were cries and moans from our folk. For despite the burning of the farms, we had all gone on hoping in the depths of our foolish hearts that the British would change their minds, that we would be allowed to go home.

I sprang up the hatch ladder, with Belle and Zachary on my heels. Overhead, canvas snapped and cracked as the sails caught the wind. The ship glided out of the mouth of Rivière Gaspereau, turning north toward the red cliffs of Cap Baptiste. A seaman shouted at us, but we clung, all three, to the railing. A sudden shaft of sunshine parted the lowering clouds, sweeping across the woods and the orchard where our dear home once stood, but no more. Like the finger of God, the light touched the steeple of the church, still unburnt, with the golden sweep of *la grand'prée* before it. Then a curtain of fog rolled in from the bay, and in a moment everything vanished like a dream.

Le 28 octobre 1755

Already the friendly cliffs of Cap Baptiste lie far behind us. We are out in la baie Française, in the middle of a great fleet of ships. All of them are carrying our people away from their homes to far shores. I had not known there were so many of us. A sailor told me that the ships carry folk from Beaubassin and Pigiguit as well as Grand-Pré, all like us torn up by the roots and dragged away. Folk from Port-Royal will follow soon. *Les Anglais sont très cruels!*

Three warships guard the fleet, circling and keeping the transports in line, just as Griffon used to herd our cows. *Mon pauvre* Griffon! I am trying very, very hard to believe he is with Jeremy.

Le 29 octobre 1755

Our hearts are wrung. Dearest Mémère has died. For days now she has not known us and last night she went to sleep and did not wake up. Maman does not weep! She said only that Mémère's soul was rooted in Acadia. Torn from her heart's land, how could she live?

Maman's dry, desperate eyes frighten me.

Le 30 octobre 1755

Today Mémère was — not buried. Not laid beside Grand-père Anselme under the willows in the churchyard where she always said she would rest. No. Instead, sailors came and wrapped her body in canvas and carried it up on deck on a plank. There was no priest to say the burial service. But the captain read words in English over her. Then they slid her body over the railing into the cold grey sea. Claude bit his lip, and Belle and Zachary and I sobbed. But still Maman does not weep.

Le 31 octobre 1755

All day Maman sat staring into space. She would eat nothing. Belle and I kept the twins, and Claude looked after Zachary. He begged a bit of rope from a sailor and taught Zachary all kinds of knots. At last Belle and I could think of no more games, and the twins grew fretful. They scrambled away from us and clung about Maman, patting her face and calling to her. Then, as if by a miracle, she roused herself and hugged them close. And then she wept at last.

Le 1ᵉʳ novembre 1755

It is as if Maman has been away on a far journey, but has come back to us. Now I can admit the terrible fear that has gnawed at me these last days. We have lost Victor and Papa, and now Mémère. But how could we survive without Maman?

She talked to Belle and me about Mémère today. It seemed to ease her heart. I was glad, for talking seemed to bring Mémère closer. No one I know well has ever died before — I was too young to remember when Grand-père Anselme died. Losing Mémère has left a big hole in my heart. I cannot believe I will never feel her kiss on my forehead again or listen to her tales on a winter's night. She will always be in my prayers. I know she is looking down from Heaven and loving us still.

Le 2 novembre 1755

The sea is much rougher now. Claude says it is because we have passed beyond la baie Française into the open ocean. The timbers of the ship groan and creak as it rolls, and the heaving does something nasty to my stomach. I

Plus tard:

I suddenly had to scramble up the ladder and hang over the railing, throwing up. Belle came after me, her face a queer shade of green, and threw up too. And we were the lucky ones. Others could not get on deck in time, or the sailors drove them back below. And so the hold now stinks worse than ever. Zachary teased Belle and me, but then the ship rolled some more and it was his turn to run for the ladder. Luckily Maman and the twins do not feel sick. Claude says they have sturdy sea legs. I do not!

Le 3 novembre 1755

On and on we sail, with never a sight of land. Where, *where* can they be taking us? I heard Maman trying to cheer Belle, telling her that perhaps we shall see all our friends and relatives at the end of the voyage. But I remember that Jeremy said the ships would go to different ports. Still, I said nothing. Why spoil a hopeful thought?

Le 4 novembre 1755

Claude has been talking to the sailors. They were surprised he knew so much English. He told them how he used to work on fishing vessels, some of them from New England. They told him we are being taken to Annapolis. When I heard that, my heart leaped for a moment because I thought he meant the Annapolis that is in Acadia, for the British call our town of Port-Royal by that name. *Mais, non.* This Annapolis is in a place called Maryland. That means *Pays de Marie.* Such a pretty name! But it is far away, farther even than Boston, where the trading ships used to come from. Claude does not know how long it will take to get there.

Les Terreurs are running wild, playing with other children. Maman lets them. After all, what harm can befall them here? And it is good not to have them clambering over me all the time!

Le 5 novembre 1755

We have survived a terrible tempest. Yesterday the ship began to roll and heave far worse than it had ever done before. Then it heeled right over on one side and water poured down the hatch before the sailors could slam it shut. We were drenched with icy salt water. It was fearful being shut in below deck in the dark, with cold water sloshing under us and no way to get out if the ship sank. The pitching and tossing made us sick all over again. People wept and moaned and prayed, and the children screamed in terror. During the height of the storm, a sailor opened the hatch and shouted for Claude to come up. They needed another hand to manage the sails. Later Claude said it was the worst storm he had ever seen.

I am a mass of bruises from where I was flung against the timbers of the hull. Today the wind is less, and we have bailed out most of the water that got in. We are not allowed up on deck for exercise, for the waves are still high.

This poor diary got splashed with seawater in the storm. I dried it out as best I could, but some pages are damp. I will not give up writing. It is all I have to cling to, now.

Le 6 novembre 1755

The stench here below is almost unbearable. *Grâce à Dieu*, they let us up on deck today to take turns breathing fresh air. I looked about for the other ships but could see none. Claude says the fleet has probably been scattered by the storm, and that damaged ships would make for nearby ports for repairs. What nearby ports? I can see nothing but the terrible heaving grey sea as far as the horizon! Pray God no poor souls drowned in the tempest!

Marie-Josèphe asked Belle and me to save our apple cores for her. She must want them for some game. I have been eating all of mine, I am so hungry.

Le 7 novembre 1755

Claude gets on well with the sailors now that they understand how much he knows about ships. They told him that Maryland is not such a bad place, and that there are many Catholic people there who worship God in the way that we do. The thought of that heartens me. Perhaps they will be kind to us! Oh, how I hope so!

Le 8 novembre 1755

Today I saw land! My heart leaped, for surely any place will be better than the hold of the *Leynord*. But my hopes were soon dashed. Claude said we are still too far north for it to be Maryland, and that I must have seen the great headland south of Boston. He says the New Englanders call it Cape Cod — that means *Cap Morue* in French. He saw it once on a sailing chart, though he has never been there.

Les Terreurs are still saving apple cores. They collect them from our neighbours, too. By now they have a goodly store put by in a bag.

Plus tard:

Jean-Baptiste Melanson comes over to chat with Claude now. He is only a little younger, and it is good for Claude to have a friend.

Le 9 novembre 1755

Daily I thank *le bon Dieu* for this diary, salt-stained as it is. It is the only thing I have of my own now, save the clothes I stand up in, my quilt bag, and my little pocket knife. Even when I am not writing I keep the diary near me. Somehow the feel of it comforts me. All our dear, lost life is between its covers. I read back over what I wrote before all these terrible things happened, and it seemed like a glimpse of Heaven. If only the words could fly off the page and make everything the way it used to be! When I came to the part about Catherine's wedding, I found the sprig of apple blossom I pressed to remember the day. Oh, where is dear Catherine now? I pray that her Basile is with her.

Le 10 novembre 1755

It is a month now since I have lived on the *Leynord*. Though what we do is not really living, just existing. We have seen no more of our little band of ships. The sailors tell Claude that some were going to a place called New York, and others to Philadelphia. Other ships besides the *Leynord* were supposed to go to Maryland. Oh, how I hope that is true, and that the Le Blancs' ship is among them. Then we will see dear Catherine again.

May we reach the Pays de Marie soon! People are ill from the voyage and the storm, and some have gone like Mémère to graves in the sea. The saddest of all the deaths was a baby. We all wept as the small canvas-wrapped bundle slid under the waves. Even the sailors looked sorry.

Le 11 novembre 1755

When Belle and I are not helping Maman with the twins, we like to curl up together and talk about everything in the world, just as Geneviève and I used to do. *Chère* Geneviève! I wonder where she is now, and the other *cousines*, too.

I used to think Belle was too young and silly to be interesting, but I was wrong. She may look delicate, but inside she is a strong person, really, like Maman. She is nearly twelve now and I am almost thirteen. Why was it so hard for me to learn to be friends with my sister? She used to tattle to Maman, it is true. But I suppose that was because I was mean to her. And *that* was because I was envious. She is so beautiful and everyone says so. And I, *hélas*, am not. I told her that, and said I was sorry for it. And I told her it was her blue eyes that saved me when I was left behind. Tears rolled down her cheeks when she heard that, and her wonderful eyes looked like blue sky under water.

Le 12 novembre 1755

Belle says if she is like Maman, I am like Papa. If only it were true! Papa always made the best of things when others were complaining. Well, from now on I will try to be more like him! I will keep my sorrows and fears for this diary and try to cheer up the others. And Belle says she never really minded when I called her Sausage. Maybe not, but I was wicked to call her so. I feel different now. I suppose our great trouble has changed us all.

Jean-Baptiste visits with us often. It is amazing how much nicer he is than Jehanne. And better-looking, too.

Plus tard:

We have had a war! This afternoon I heard *les Terreurs* giggling together. I saw Josèph-Marie nudging Blaise Terriot, who is right beside us. Then suddenly the air was full of flying apple cores. From every corner of the ship's hold they came, pelting down around us. And *les Terreurs* and the Terriot boy were firing back. The little wretches must have planned the whole thing with other mischief makers.

Well, old Simon Terriot was dozing after the

midday meal. An apple core hit him smack on the nose and he woke up, snorting. Then he started yelling. And no wonder, for his temper is not sunny at the best of times. To my amazement, Maman burst out laughing, so Belle and I did too. By the time Maman wiped her eyes and collared the twins they were out of ammunition anyway. All the little troublemakers were set to picking up the cores. Claude took half a sackful up on deck to dump over the side. Maman gave the twins a scolding, of course. But not a serious one.

How long has it been since we have laughed like that?

Le 13 novembre 1755

I dreamed last night that we were home in Acadia, harvesting the apples. It was a beautiful golden day. Zachary had climbed up into a tree, and Belle and I were filling baskets with the ripe red fruit he tossed into our aprons. Papa was pressing some for cider, and joking with Victor that he was old enough now to taste it once it was fermented. The smell of crushed apple was so strong that it woke me. For a moment I lay, dazed, not understanding where I was, for the apple smell still clung about me. Then I felt under my quilt bag, which I use for a pillow, and came upon an apple core. It must have rolled there during the apple war. I lay in the dark with tears running down my cheeks as I thought of all we have left behind, and of our dear Papa and Victor and Catherine and Mémère, all lost to us forever.

Le 14 novembre 1755

Every day our ration of tough boiled beef and hard bread gets a little smaller. We got no apples today, nor any vegetable but turnips. People mutter that provisions are getting low, and worry about whether we will reach Maryland before they run out. Claude says the storm must have driven us far off course.

Le 15 novembre 1755

Today I was chewing on a piece of stale bread when I noticed something *wiggling* in it. It was full of fat white maggots! I screamed, but Claude said maggots never hurt anyone, and that I should just think of them as extra rations. Ugh!

I noticed the twins stuffing bits of bread in their pockets, so I kept a sharp eye on them to see what new mischief they were up to. I spied them laying out the bread near a little hole in the ship's timber. Lo and behold, a small grey rat soon poked its nose out, and began to nibble the bread. Not wanting to alarm Maman and Belle, I scooped the twins up and whispered that rats are nasty and dirty and NOT TO BE PLAYED WITH. Just as seriously, they told me that this was a *good* rat, and that his name is Bonhomme Gris. Poor things — they are missing their pets as I miss Griffon. I made them promise solemnly not to touch the rat and said no more.

Le 16 novembre 1755

Jehanne has been ill since the storm. Kind-hearted Belle feels sorry for her, and so we go to sit with her sometimes. I think so many ill things about Jehanne that I really should try to find something good to say about her. Here it is — she is forthright. She says just what she thinks. The bad thing is that what she says is as sharp as the quills of a *porc-épic*. Lately her illness has softened her tongue, but today she said something spiteful about Marie Hébert, so she must be getting better. Jean-Baptiste thanked us for visiting her. *He* is always pleasant-spoken.

Le 17 novembre 1755

Jehanne does not like my diary. No one in her family can read or write, and she thinks it is all a great vanity. She said so yesterday. I am cross with her and will not visit her today. I do not see why my diary is her business. Sometimes I think *le bon Dieu* has put Jehanne here to punish me. I try to guard my tongue and stay cheerful, but she does not make it easy.

Even though they cannot read and write, Jehanne's family are luckier than we are, for they are all together. I know Victor is lost to us forever, but I try to believe that we will see Papa again some day. But in my heart I fear it cannot be so. Maman says *le bon Dieu* brought Claude back to us after all, and we must place our trust in Him. I do try. But my mind scurries from one fear to the next, like Bonhomme Gris hunting for crumbs.

Plus tard:

Jehanne is better. She got up and came over to say she was sorry that she had said things about my diary. She says she can see how it helps me pass the time. It is a wonder — I do not think Jehanne has ever said "sorry" before. She offered to show Belle a new stitch for her knitting, too.

Le 18 novembre 1755

Now Belle has fallen ill. She coughs and shivers. We have bundled her up in every spare piece of clothing we own and wrapped her in Claude's heavy cloak. But still she shivers. I trust she has only caught a cold, and no wonder in this damp ship!

The *Leynord* creaks and groans as it thrashes through the waves. The sailors told Claude the captain is making as much sail as the masts can carry to speed our journey.

Le 19 novembre 1755

The ship is turning! This morning when I went up on deck the rising sun was on my right-hand side. (I mean, to starboard. Claude has been teaching us proper ship's language.) So we must be heading north again. Could they be taking us back to Acadia?

Plus tard:

No. *Les Anglais* will never take us home. Claude was on deck and he says we have turned the point of another great headland and are sailing up a long narrow bay with low land stretching away on both sides. He thinks it may be the bay of the Pays de Marie! Can we really be getting close to the end of our journey?

Le 20 novembre 1755

In the middle of the night, a great rattle of chain awoke us, followed by a splash. The ship swung around and suddenly the lively feel of it beneath us went dull and dead. People sat up, alarmed, and there was a babble of questions. Claude called out that there was nothing to fear — the ship had just dropped anchor. People settled down again, but I doubt that many of us slept. I know I did not.

People pushed and shoved trying to go on deck first this morning. Even Belle was eager to see this Maryland they have brought us to. But there is not much to see, just some low snow-covered hills under a leaden sky, and a small village huddled by the bay. What is more exciting is that another ship rides at anchor not far off. Claude recognized it — it is the *Elizabeth*, from Grand-Pré too! When people heard that their eyes clung to the ship, wondering if one of their lost ones might be aboard. For everyone here has lost someone.

Belle is no better.

Le 21 novembre 1755

This village of Annapolis looks not much bigger than Grand-Pré, and now two ships full of strangers have arrived. I wonder if anyone told the people we were coming? Will they be kind to us and help us? I fear that they will not!

Le 22 novembre 1755

People are muttering and wondering why we cannot go ashore. There is no real food at all now, just thin soup with a few scraps of stringy beef. Even the water is almost gone, and what is left is slimy. It is disgusting to have to drink it!

Le 23 novembre 1755

Nothing is happening. Longboats scuttle back and forth between the ship and the village, but still they do not let us go ashore.

Les Terreurs are excited about Annapolis. But they do not want to leave Bonhomme Gris behind. I overheard them planning to smuggle him ashore when we go! I explained — very quietly, so no one else would hear — that Bonhomme Gris is better off where he is. It is his home, after all. I added that we did not like being taken from *our* home, did we? At this their eyes grew very round, and they promised to leave him where he is.

Plus tard:

Belle still coughs and shivers. I am worried — she should be getting over a cold by now. I could not bear it if — no! I will not even think it!

Le 24 novembre 1755

They have brought us a barrel of fresh water. I had forgotten that water could taste so good! But it comes too late for some of us. Many are ill with fevers and stomach complaints.

Le 25 novembre 1755

Our menfolk went to see the captain. Claude translated for them — I am so proud of him! The men begged the captain to let us go ashore, as people are ill from lack of food. The captain says that the Governor of Maryland is away, and he cannot unload his passengers until he returns. He is trying to buy supplies from the village. What a muddle *les Anglais* have made of things!

Le 27 novembre 1755

The notches on the timber tell me that it is a month now since we left Grand-Pré. It seems longer, like years, and we have all changed. Maman looks older, and today as she braided her hair I saw threads of grey glinting in it. Claude has become very grave. It is hard being the man of the family. *Pauvre* Claude — he is only sixteen! Belle is terribly thin and pale now, with dark circles under her eyes. Zachary seems to have forgotten his mischief. Only *les Terreurs* are as lively as ever. Not even *les Anglais* have squelched those two!

Et moi? I feel dull and slow, my spirit as cramped as our bodies are. I look at the shore and my courage almost fails me. How will we find the strength to face what awaits us there? Yet if they keep us longer aboard we will surely die.

Le 28 novembre 1755

When, oh when, will they let us go ashore? It *must* be soon. Yet I dread what is to come. I have no heart to write more.

Le 29 novembre 1755

Belle slept a great deal today, tossing and moaning. Maman watches her closely. I noticed a little colour in Belle's cheeks and thought she must be better. I told Maman, hoping to cheer her, but she just shook her head. She says Belle has a low fever. The dirt and darkness and poor food of the ship have made her sick. Once we are ashore she will get well again, I know it!

Le 30 novembre 1755

Two more ships have come into the harbour! Claude thinks they too were at Grand-Pré. *Les Anglais* have done us a great wrong. But at least they have brought some of us to the same place. Soon we will see our friends and some may even find their dear ones! I wish I could dare to dream that Papa may be among them. *Mais, non.* He could not be, for he was in Halifax, not Grand-Pré. But perhaps *le bon Dieu* will return Catherine to us!

Le 1er décembre 1755

It is too cruel! This afternoon the three other ships hoisted sail and moved out of the harbour.

Our eyes clung to them as they vanished from sight — one to the north, around a headland, and the others back down the bay. The *Leynord* is left alone, and our hearts are aching.

Le 2 décembre 1755

Sailors say the townsfolk of Annapolis complained about so many ships full of people. They do not want strangers among them. And so the other ships will drop their passengers at different places. We do not know where. How can we bear this?

Le 3 décembre 1755

The men among us gather in little groups, and voices are raised in anger. We are dying of dirt and hunger. We would not treat animals the way *les Anglais* are treating us. Claude went to talk to the sailors, and some of them agree that the captain cannot keep us here longer. Does he want us all to die?

Le 4 décembre 1755

We are going ashore! Here is how it happened. There was a kind of revolt, and our men stormed up on deck. Zachary and I peeked over the top of the hatch to see what would happen. Claude and the others set to work to lower the longboats. The sailors did not help them, but they did not hinder them either. Then the captain came up on deck with two soldiers, who pointed their weapons at our men. After a moment, though, he ordered them to lower their weapons. He told Claude and the others that if the Governor has not returned by tomorrow, he himself will have the longboats lowered and will send us ashore. He gave his word on it. If he is an honest man, tonight will be our last night in this horrible ship.

I count over the notches in the ship's rib. I have lived here for fifty-eight endless days.

Le 6 décembre 1755
Annapolis

I have much to tell. We are in the strangest place — a kind of shed with a sloping roof. It is attached to the back of a small wooden house. Mistress Finnerty says this kind of house is called a salt box. But I must explain who she is, and what has happened.

The captain kept his word. When no order came from the governor, he sent us ashore in the longboats yesterday. It was cold, with a cutting wind and a flurry of snow in the air. We huddled on the dock, waiting until all our people were brought from the ship. Then, carrying our few bundles of possessions, we trudged after a troop of blue-coated soldiers into the town. It is a little place of wooden houses grouped about the harbour. In the centre is a sort of square, and here the soldiers marched us. Curious folk stood round about, eyeing us as if we were a pack of wolves straight from the woods. An official read a long proclamation. I did not understand every word, but it said that we Acadians were cast upon the charity of the local people, that they must give us food and find us places to stay. Later, the government would decide what to do with us.

An angry murmur ran through the crowd. The faces of the people were hard and closed, and they looked as though they hated us. When I whispered that to Claude, he nodded. He said that these people are fighting against France in the West, and that to them, all French people are enemies. Belle coughed, and leaned against my shoulder, and I felt such despair as I had never felt before.

Then a plump woman in a woollen cloak stepped forward. I gazed into her bright brown eyes and found no hatred there, only pity. And I saw that she wore a cross like mine around her neck. She said her name was Mistress Finnerty, and that we were to go home with her!

And so we did. Mistress Finnerty has given us a place in her shed, and though it is cold, there are quilts to bundle ourselves in, and tallow candles for light. Before anything, though, she sat us down around her kitchen table and put big bowls of steaming *ragoût* before us. There were lumps of a strange white vegetable in it. I held a bit on my spoon, and asked Mistress Finnerty what it was. She looked astonished that I knew it not, and said it was called "potato." It is delicious, and I said so. She nodded, well pleased, as all of us emptied our bowls. Even Belle ate more than she has done for many days.

It is too dark to write more.

Le 7 décembre 1755

This morning Claude and Zachary set to work helping Mistress Finnerty, to try to repay her charity toward us. They cleared away snowbanks from around her door, then they chopped a mountain of firewood, and filled the cauldron on the hearth with fresh water from the well. But none of that made Master Finnerty like us any the better. He is a hard man and he is angry at his wife for giving us shelter. He says it serves him right for marrying a Papist. I asked Claude what a Papist was, and he said it was people like us who worshipped God in the Catholic Church. Most British people are called Protestants. The God they worship is the same as ours, but Claude says they worship Him differently. I wonder if *le bon Dieu* likes one kind of worship better than another.

Le 8 décembre 1755

Today Claude and Zachary went about the town trying to get a bit of work to do and also to pick up news about our people. It seems that Mistress Finnerty set a good example, and other folk came forward to help some of the Acadian families. The rest are staying in the church until people decide what to do.

It is truly a great muddle. Claude says the townspeople did not know how many Acadians would come. They are very angry that so many of us have been brought here. That is why the other ships were sent away. I try not to think about them or to wonder who might be on them.

Maman is caring for Belle and the twins, and I

try to be useful to Mistress Finnerty. She has her loom set up for the winter and asked if I was a good weaver. I confessed that I was not, that Belle was much better at it. Still, I will do my best, for she is so good to us. I try to keep out of the way of Master Finnerty, though. He has orange hair just like Jeremy's, but his eyes are green and cold as pebbles, and he likes us not.

Le 9 décembre 1755

I have been looking at a strange thing called a newspaper. Claude brought it from the village. It is like a book, but much thinner. Claude says people buy it to read about things that happen. I could see the words *French neutrals* dotted around on the front page. So I set myself to read a bit of it. It was very hard, but I understood some of it. I am sorry that I did! The newspaper said terrible things about us — that Acadians are thieves, robbers and murderers, and that decent folk should have nothing to do with them! My eyes filled with tears of anger as I read. How dare they tell such lies about us after all the British have made us suffer! I threw the newspaper into a corner and will read no more.

Plus tard:

I went on an errand with Mistress Finnerty, to carry her market basket. I blushed every time I felt someone's eyes on me, for they will be thinking I am a wicked person. I am not!

Le 10 décembre 1755

I am growing very fond of Mistress Finnerty. She is so very kind to all of us, and to me especially. She says she has always wanted a daughter, but God has not given her any children of her own. It is a great sorrow to her. So even after the housework is done, she has me spend much time with her, sewing and keeping her company. She is fond of the twins, too, and smuggles sweetmeats to them.

I try to go along day by day, and not think what may come tomorrow. For things cannot stay as they are. Master Finnerty's angry gaze tells me that. He is a *nasty* man!

Le 11 décembre 1755

Belle is much worse. Kind Mistress Finnerty has dosed her with all her favourite remedies, but nothing seems to help. Last night Belle's breathing became rough and heavy, and in a panic I rushed around to the front door and pounded on it. Master Finnerty came down in his nightcap and shouted at me to go away, but Mistress Finnerty called out asking what was wrong. She had us bring Belle into the house and bedded her down in the warmest spot before the fire. Then she boiled a kettle of water and after a while the steam seemed to ease Belle's breathing.

Maman whispered a blessing, and I told Mistress Finnerty what she had said. The two of them hugged each other. If only all the British were like kind Mistress Finnerty!

Le 12 décembre 1755

Belle grows no better. Claude ran all about the town trying to find a doctor who would visit her. At last one came. He is a grumpy old man with bushy eyebrows, but he was very gentle with Belle. When he had examined her, though, he shook his head. He told Claude that she has a grave affliction of the lungs. All we can do is keep her warm and dose her with a medicine he will give us. He scribbled something on a piece of paper and bade Claude take it right away to an *apothicaire* nearby who makes medicines. When Claude offered him the few coins he has managed to earn the doctor waved them away.

So Belle lies close to the fire in Mistress Finnerty's kitchen, and I keep vigil beside her, warding off the spiteful glances of Master Finnerty. He stomps about complaining of "plague-ridden French."

Le 13 décembre 1755

I am writing this in the middle of the night. Maman is worn out and I made her go to rest for a while. Belle lies in a stupor, struggling to breathe. It is as if she is drowning. The medicine has done no good. I have prayed and prayed for her to get better, but she does not. Surely God will not take her from us!

Plus tard:

Oh, Belle! My heart is breaking. I cannot bear it. I *cannot*! Not *this*, too! Just a little while ago, Belle opened her eyes. She knew me. For the first time in days! She smiled up at me — such a sweet smile. The pain and weariness of the fever seemed gone. I squeezed her hand joyfully. I was so sure she was better. Then she closed her eyes, the bluest in all Acadia, and gave a little sigh. And then

No, I cannot write the word. I cannot!

Le 14 décembre 1755

The twins cry and cry — they loved Belle so. Zachary tries to hide his tears, for he wants to be grown-up now. But his eyes are swollen and red. Maman and Claude are strong and try to console the rest of us. As for me, my heart is like a stone. I will not forgive God for letting Belle die. I cannot.

Claude and Zachary have made a coffin from some planks Mistress Finnerty has given us. She grieves with us. She promises that a priest will say the funeral service for Belle, and this comforts us a little.

When no one was looking I cut a little square from the hem of Belle's blue dress and folded it away in my quilt bag. Now she will always be with me.

Le 15 décembre 1755

We buried Belle today. Acadian men came to help Claude dig the grave in the Catholic churchyard, and our people stood in silence while Father Howard read the burial service. He is a very different sort of priest from our dear Père Chauvreulx, but the words were in Latin, so they sounded just the same as they did at home. The half-frozen clods of earth thumped down on the lid of the coffin as the men filled in the grave. Of course there were no flowers to strew. How could there be in bleak winter? So we had to leave Belle under a heap of raw earth. It looked so lonely.

Jehanne and Jean-Baptiste came over afterward with Madame Melanson and said how sad they were to hear about Belle. I hope Jehanne remembers some of the mean things she said about Belle and is sorry for them now. When I said that to Maman, she said I must try to be more charitable. That when we are sorrowing, our neighbours are our help and support. *Hélas*, I suppose she is right.

Le 16 décembre 1755

After the service yesterday, the men stood talking a while. It was the first time many of us have been together since getting off the ship. There was much muttering and shaking of heads. It seems the Governor's Council has issued a new proclamation. Some of us will be sent away from Annapolis. When we told Mistress Finnerty she said she would keep us, come what may.

But then Master Finnerty came home grinning from ear to ear. Of course he brought more bad news. There was more to the governor's proclamation than we had heard. It also said no Papist can give shelter to Acadians, for fear of French plots. Why on earth would English Papists want to plot with the French? And how could helpless people like us plot anyway? But now our good Mistress Finnerty cannot keep us after all. Maman and Claude stayed up late, talking in low voices. What are we going to do now? I am afraid.

Le 17 décembre 1755

Today Claude came back from the town with hopeful news. A ship from a place called Baltimore has come into the harbour. A man there has heard about us Acadians, and has offered to find a place there for fifty of us. Claude thinks we should go, for we cannot stay where we are — we might bring misfortune on Mistress Finnerty. But to have to go on another ship! At first Maman said no, absolutely. But Claude persuaded her at last. Baltimore is not far — less than a day's sail. And the ship is small and fast. The captain came ashore to talk to the town council. Any Acadians who wish to go must present themselves at the harbour tomorrow morning. And so we are going to go. What none of us says aloud is how it tears our hearts to leave Belle behind.

Le 18 décembre 1755
Baltimore

Mistress Finnerty saw us off this morning with many tears and a hamper full of food to help us on our way. She had already given us some castoff clothes. And a good thing too — some of ours were only fit for burning. At least we do not quite look like beggars now! At the harbour we saw some of the people we knew from the *Leynord*. *Les* Melanson were among them. Jean-Baptiste looked very happy to see us. But Jehanne had eyes only for our hamper. She is always on the lookout for something to her advantage, that one. Maman saw her staring, too, and said we must share what we have like good Acadians. So I passed over some loaves and potted meat. Jehanne blushed, but took them willingly enough. Jean-Baptiste nodded his thanks.

Claude was right about the voyage — it was nothing at all. Just a quick run up the bay before a stiff breeze. In the afternoon we anchored in Baltimore harbour. Baltimore is a much bigger place than Annapolis, and at first I felt a little frightened. There are many sturdy red brick buildings that seemed to frown upon us as we came ashore. But Master Andrew Stygar, the man who had us brought here, met us on the quay. I write this at his house. For he and other kind folk have promised to shelter us for a few days. And he says he has a plan for after that. We will find out about it tomorrow.

Every night I put my rosary under my pillow, but I do not say my prayers. I cannot, since Belle died.

Le 19 décembre 1755

Master Andrew's plan is wonderful! He says we Acadians will have our very own house. At least, we will if he can persuade the town council to let us use an abandoned one he has found. How I hope he succeeds, for to live on our own again would be wonderful. Maman's weary eyes lit up when Claude told her, and she asked him to thank Master Andrew from the bottom of her heart. When Claude explained what she had said, Master Andrew gave her a funny little bow. He is a kind man, I think, though not a handsome one. His nose is snub and turns up at the end. It gives him a very *drôle* look.

Le 20 décembre 1755

Master Andrew's plan is going to work! The mayor and select men of the town have given their permission. Now we must set about cleaning the old house. Master Andrew said perhaps we can move in by Christmas. Christmas! I had completely forgotten about it. For a moment the thought gave me a dreadful pang. I cannot help thinking of all the wonderful preparations we would have been making at home. But I must try not to brood about it. At least we will be busy now, not sitting about waiting for orders.

Le 21 décembre 1755

Today we saw our new home for the first time. It is in the oldest part of town, not far from the harbour, and the streets round about are paved with queer roundish stones. It is very different from the kind of house we are used to, and has many rooms upstairs as well as downstairs. Master Andrew had warned us that the house was old and rundown, but seeing it was still a shock. The windows were boarded over, and there were holes in the roof. Maman and the other women exchanged horrified glances, and burst out into a babble of protest. Inside, they poked about, exclaiming in disgust at the dirt and cobwebs from years of neglect. The men stomped on the floors and rapped on the walls and shook their heads doubtfully.

Pauvre Master Andrew looked a bit crestfallen. Yet soon enough the women were demanding brooms and the men were discussing how many planks and shingles would be needed. We Acadians like to have our say, *pour sûr*! But we soon roll up our sleeves and get to work!

Le 22 décembre 1755

All day long we have slaved away at the house. I am stiff and aching for it is long since any of us have done a day's hard work. But already the place is much cleaner. And Master Andrew got merchants of the town to help out with shingles to patch the roof and planks to mend the worst holes in the floor.

Now people are arguing about who will live in which room, for there will have to be more than one family in each. And the women will have to share a common kitchen. Claude said, with a wink, that feathers will fly for sure, for every housewife likes to run her own kitchen. I hope we do not have to share our room with *les* Melanson.

Jehanne will poke her sharp nose into everything!

One thing everyone agrees upon, though, is that we must set aside one room for a chapel. We picked out a nice one with a tall window, and whitewashed the walls to freshen it. Now we will ask a priest to consecrate it for us. For surely people here, even Papist ones, will not want us to attend their churches.

Le 23 décembre 1755

Behind all our excitement about the house lurks a fear about how we can make a living here. We are farmers, after all. And what use is a farmer in a town? The men talk much about it, saying that the British should treat us as prisoners of war. After all, they took away our land and shipped us to this foreign place. So should they not help support us? But Claude says we should be too proud to take anything more from *les Anglais* than we have to. Already he has been down to the harbour, and has picked up work on the docks. Zachary goes with him, and helps out as best he can.

I think much upon this, for I long to earn money for the family too. Master Andrew has a little housemaid named Susanna. She is about my age, and I watch her go about her tasks. Perhaps I could do that kind of work. But when I mentioned this to Maman, she frowned and snapped that Acadians are not servants.

I try to stay excited about our new house. But sometimes I feel shut in here among so many buildings, and long for the wide sky and the open fields. And I miss Belle. I still do not say my prayers at night. At family prayers I just move my lips. I suppose I am wicked, but I do not think God cares about us. If He did, He would not have let Belle die.

Today, on the way to the new house I saw a dog. It was big and shaggy like *pauvre* Griffon. I got a big lump in my throat that would not go away. My faithful Griffon! Where is he now? With Jeremy, I pray. Perhaps he has even forgotten me. I try not to think so.

Le 24 décembre 1755

It is Christmas Eve, and today we moved into our new house. Luckily, not all the Acadians who came to Baltimore want to live here, or we would be even more crowded. Still, we do have to share a room with *les* Melanson. Maman knows well how I feel about Jehanne. She says living with her is a cross *le bon Dieu* wishes me to bear. *Why?*

It is hard not to think of how things would be back home. There would be crisp snow instead of this soggy kind. At night we would drive to the church in sleighs, dressed in our very best. And there would be a manger scene and the soft glow of honey-smelling beeswax candles. And dear Père Chauvreulx would say Mass. I wonder where he is now, *pauvre homme!*

Le 25 décembre 1755

Yesterday evening we fasted until midnight, then took candles and went and knelt in the chapel. We had no priest, but people said their rosaries. I did not, until Maman gave me a sharp glance. After that I pretended. And then we sang a hymn.

This morning Master Andrew brought a priest to consecrate our chapel. It was good of him to think of us on his own Christmas Day. Father Wentworth seems a kind man. He blessed our little chapel, and said Mass. People wept, for it was the first time we had heard Mass for many months. I wish I could feel God near me, but I cannot. It is a lonely feeling.

Father Wentworth said he would come back

sometimes, but that we should come to his church too. But I think most people will be too shy to go, because *les Anglais* like us not.

For dinner the women made a great *fricot* with the best of our provisions, our first real meal in our new house.

Le 26 décembre 1755

Today I did a very bold thing. Maman does not know yet. I plucked up my courage and went around to the back door of Master Andrew's house and asked for Susanna. When she came I asked her how to get work like hers in the town. She said her parents had found it for her. So I was no better off. After that, I went around to the front door and asked for Master Andrew. He was most surprised to see me by myself. I told him what I wanted, and he rubbed his chin. He says that not many would want to employ a French girl, but that my English might help. He will see what he can do.

I will not say anything to Maman and Claude until I hear from Master Andrew. It will be a happy surprise for them.

Le 27 décembre 1755

Why do I always see things right when it is too late? Of course I should have asked Maman's permission before seeking work. But I did not, and now I am in disgrace. This evening, Master Andrew came round to the door in his carriage and asked to speak to Maman and Claude. He told them what I had asked, and that he had found me work in the house of a friend of his who needed a scullery maid. When Claude had translated for Maman, her face flushed and her eyes shot sparks at me. Then she asked Claude to tell Master Andrew that I could not go. But Claude said I should be allowed to try it. And so at last she agreed that I could see how the work went. But after Master Andrew had gone, she said I was never to do something so underhanded again.

I am truly sorry Maman is angry. But underneath I am a little proud of myself, too, for finding work to help my family.

Le 28 décembre 1755

I was not sure what a scullery maid was, but now I know. It means working in the kitchen washing mountains of dirty dishes and greasy pots. It is a task I have always hated, but I will not give up. Master Andrew's friend is called Master Hardcastle, and he has a fine house with many servants. The only good thing about working in the hot smelly kitchen is that there is plenty of food. Today they sent me home with a basket full of good things. Maman shared it out with as many people as we could. Jehanne says it is a low thing to wash someone else's dishes. But still she took her share from the basket!

Oh, I almost forgot. Such a strange thing has happened. I was helping Maman empty a wash-tub the other day and drenched my apron. My diary was in the pocket and I whisked it out to save it another soaking. But the willow twig I keep inside it dropped into the soapy water. I fished it out and put it on the windowsill to dry. Today the buds on it look swollen, and Maman says if I plant it, it may take root.

Le 29 décembre 1755

I got home very late, as there was a *fête* today *chez* Hardcastle and many dishes to be washed. My hands were red and swollen from the hot water and strong soap. But the cook praised me for not breaking anything, and again sent me off with a basket of good things. Maman put a plate of *ragoût* before me. When I almost fell asleep eating it, she put her arms around me and said I was her *brave fille*, and that she was proud of me, and sorry that she had been cross. Then she sighed and said that our world was different now and that we must change with it. She even said she was thinking how to find some work for herself!

It is the very first time Maman has spoken to me as if I were a grown-up. It makes me feel very proud.

Le 30 décembre 1755

Master Andrew says he will help Maman find laundry and sewing to do. And Madame Melanson and Jehanne have promised to watch Marie-Josèphe and Josèph-Marie while she is busy. So all of us have work now. Claude and Zachary were very surprised about Maman's work. The four of us shook hands. We Richards vowed to show Baltimore what hard work is!

Le 31 décembre 1755

More trouble! But at least this time I am not to blame. I was not needed at Master Hardcastle's until the afternoon today, so this morning I went with Maman to help her carry back a big basket of laundry from a house nearby. When we came down the street nearest our house, we heard voices singing in French. Then we saw Marie-Josèphe and Josèph-Marie standing hand in hand on the corner. They were singing songs and holding out a tin cup. People passing by were tossing pennies into it! Maman swooped down on the twins and shooed them before her into the house. I picked up the laundry, which had tumbled into the gutter and got even dirtier.

Inside, people gathered around us. *Les Terreurs* bawled as Maman tried to get the truth out of them. It seems that the idea was Marie-Josèphe's — it almost always is. They had slipped off when Madame Melanson was not looking. Maman was overcome with shame that people would think we were beggars.

I pleaded with her that the twins only wanted to work like the rest of us. At this, Marie-Josèphe held out a grubby handful of pennies, sobbing that they sang very well, and people had paid them for it. Maman's expression softened. The twins in trouble — it was so *ordinaire*. Just like the old days. We hugged each other, first laughing, then weeping.

1756

Le 1er janvier 1756

It is New Year's Day. I cannot help looking backward with longing. We were so happy this time last year! The thought of us all together — Papa and Catherine, Victor and Mémère and Belle — closes my throat with tears. Maman mourns, too. But somehow she manages to be grateful to *le bon Dieu* for what we have left. Claude, too, is his sweet-souled self. It seems that only I cannot accept what has befallen us.

Of course we cannot celebrate as we used to do, though Maman and I have worked in secret on small presents for everyone. Also, the kind cook *chez* Hardcastle gave me some sweetmeats for the children. But there will be no round of visits or fancy new linen collars and caps to show off. Yet Maman says we still have the most important part of the New Year — the feeling of hope and new beginnings. And the end of old grudges and disputes. As soon as we got up, people began greeting each other, wishing each other a happy year and Heaven at the end of our days. Women who just last night had argued about whose turn it was to use our few pots and pans now shook hands, nodding and smiling. Men who had shouted at each other over politics clapped each other on the back and smoked a pipe together.

Jean-Baptiste was the first to wish me a prosperous New Year. He grows more handsome every day, and I could not help blushing. Then I saw Jehanne coming my way. I did not know what to say to her, for truly I have never liked her, and have suffered much from her barbed tongue. She is so unlike her brother! But she spoke first, begging my pardon for anything wrong she had done. So of course I had to do the same. We shook hands and vowed to be better friends this year. Now I feel fresh-scrubbed and shiny inside. I used to think God would approve. But now I do not think He pays much attention to us. If He does, why has He let so many terrible things happen?

Le 2 janvier 1756

I was right to doubt God cares about us! Today a group of strange people came and tried to take the twins away. They spoke no French and I could only understand some of what they were saying. Voices got louder and louder until the strangers and our folk were shouting at each other. I ran for Master Andrew, and he came right away. After he had heard what the strangers had to say he looked grave. Speaking very slowly, so I could understand every word, he told us that our neighbours had reported that the twins were begging in the street, and that their parents must be neglecting them.

I told him how it had been, and Master Andrew explained to the others, but they shook their heads. Master Andrew says because we have only Maman and not Papa too, these people do not believe that we can earn enough to take care of the twins properly. It is true that they look very ragged, for they still wear the clothing stained by our terrible journey. Good Mistress Finnerty had had no children's clothes to give them. And of course they had managed to get themselves grubby since Maman had washed their hands and faces this morning.

Maman turned dead white and sank down on a bench, gathering the twins close against her. She began to weep, sobbing that *les Anglais* had no right to take away her babies. But I could see from the look on Master Andrew's face that they *could* do it if they chose. I begged him to tell them how hard we are trying, and he spoke with them a while. At last they went away. Master Andrew said that we were on "probation." I said I did not understand the word, and he explained that it means that if the twins are seen begging and if we do not give them better clothing and the best of food they will be taken away. He said they will be bound out to a family as servants for some years to work and pay for their keep. *Les Anglais* must be crazy! Our little ones are too young to work! I cannot bear to think what would become of them without us.

Plus tard:

Claude says he will somehow work two shifts to make more money. I will ask the cook if I can do extra, too. We must do *something*, for Maman is in despair.

Le 3 janvier 1756

A cloud seems to hang over us now. Everything looks so black! And there is no chance, no chance at all, that *les Anglais* will set us free to go back to our own country. At night the men sit talking about the news Claude heard down on the docks. An even greater war is coming between Britain and France. We Acadians will be hated more than ever!

Le 4 janvier 1756

I am now chopping vegetables and mopping floors *chez* Harcastle to earn a few more pennies, and Maman has taken in sewing and mending to do as well as laundry. Most evenings she sits up late, straining her eyes over the close work by the light of a smoky tallow candle. I try to help, but my work is not very neat. Oh, how I wish I had learned better what Mémère tried to teach me.

Yesterday poor Claude rose before daybreak and tramped off in the cold trying to find extra work. We could tell by his face when he came home that he did not find it. Today was no better. And though Zachary does his best he cannot earn a man's wage.

If we lose the twins it will break Maman's heart.

Le 5 janvier 1756

Jehanne came to me today and vowed that while Maman and I are busy she will never let the twins out of her sight for even a minute. I thanked her from the bottom of my heart, for if they get out on the street one more time *les Anglais* will take them from us. I am so glad that I made New Year's peace with Jehanne. And Jean-Baptiste brought a few coins he had made chopping fire-wood and insisted Maman take them to help pay for new clothes for *les Terreurs*. He is so kind!

Claude found a bit of extra work in a joinery, so at least he was inside for part of the day. But he was still half-frozen when he stumbled in this evening. I ran to warm up his supper, but by the time I put it before him he was asleep at the table with his head on his arms. I suddenly noticed how thin he is. He is not much more than a boy, after all, and now the fate of our family rests on him. I felt sick with pity.

There is only one tiny omen of good. My stubborn willow sprig has struck roots. I will keep it carefully and plant it outdoors in the spring. It is so strange to think of a bit of Acadia growing here in Baltimore!

Le 6 janvier 1756

Today is *Les Rois*, the day of the three Kings who came to see the Christ Child. To us it is just another working day, for *les Anglais* do not seem to celebrate it. At home there would have been a rich *galette de Rois*, with dried beans hidden in two portions to choose a king and queen for the *fête*. There would have been music and dancing.

But here there is just a blank nothing.

I also sorted over the patches in my quilt bag. Some of the women here have given me bits they can spare, so my collection has grown. But I have had a strange thought. Are not the scraps in my bag like we Acadians, torn away from where they belong, bundled together in a strange place? It is not a happy thought. Perhaps I will never finish my quilt after all.

There are only a few pages left in this diary. It is just as well. I scarcely have the heart to write anymore.

Le 7 janvier 1756

Something wonderful has happened! How could I ever have doubted that *le bon Dieu* has us in his care? How wicked I have been! Oh, my thoughts are as scattered as pins dropped upon the floor! I must gather them and tell how it came to pass.

Yesterday, after supper, everything was as dreary as usual. The twins were abed and Maman and I were sewing by candlelight. The men were gathered about the hearth, smoking their pipes, and groups of women sat knitting and gossiping. Snow was falling outside, quieting the noise of the town. Suddenly there came a knocking at the door. A man went to lift the latch, and a stranger stepped inside. A roughly dressed fellow with a long beard, he brushed snow off his broad shoulders. Then he pulled off his cap and asked if this was the dwelling of the Acadians.

I was only half paying attention, for folk have found their way to us before, looking for their lost ones. But Maman jumped up, her face ablaze like the full moon reflecting the sun, and cried "Michel!" The man stared wildly for a moment, then he opened his arms and Maman ran into them. He swung her around, lifting her feet right off the floor, and buried his face in her hair. It was Papa!

I hurled myself on him, and Papa hugged me close and called me his Pouliche. Claude and Zachary ran over, shouting, and Papa clapped them on the back. He has changed much, our papa, and it is not just the beard. There are deep lines in his face where there were none before, and wings of silver in his dark hair. But he is Papa all the same. Real. Ours!

At last he looked around and asked for Belle. And so we had to tell him of our dear ones who were lost. Catherine and Mémère. And Belle. Then Papa wept. It wrung our hearts to see him grieve so, and made our old sorrows knife-keen again.

Our faces wet with tears, we knelt for his blessing. For the first time in so long! And I said a special prayer of my own to *le bon Dieu*, giving thanks and begging His forgiveness.

Le 8 janvier 1756

This is the very last page of my diary, and I write these words with a full heart. Everything has changed since Papa's return and we are full of hope again. *Les Anglais* will never get our twins now! Papa is a fine carpenter, and Master Andrew has found him work at fair pay in a joiner's shop. With all of us working, there is money for our needs and to spare. Now we can help others, as good Acadians should do.

Papa brought good news with him. Oncle Paul and Tante Cécile and their family were on the same ship he was. *Ma chère* Geneviève — perhaps I shall see her again some time! The British had brought Papa back from Halifax, but they put him on the wrong ship. He and the others ended up in a place in the Pays de Marie called Oxford. They heard that other Acadians had made a home in Baltimore, and Papa decided he must come here to look for us. It has taken him all this time to walk and work his way here. We are so happy to be together again, though we never forget our dear lost ones. I do not like to think of *chère* Belle all alone in the Annapolis churchyard. I have made a vow to visit her grave and plant a little dog rose upon it to bear her company in her long sleep.

I showed my diary to Papa and he says it is wonderful that I managed to keep it through all that has happened. He says other people may read it some day, and learn what happened to our family and our people. I had not thought of that, and it makes me proud. I will put my diary away and keep it carefully. When I have a daughter some day, I will give it to her. And I will teach her how to read and write as Mémère taught me. *Pour sûr*!

She shall have my quilt, too. For I *am* going to finish it, however long it takes! It is true that we Acadians have been torn from our homes and scattered to the four winds. But perhaps, like my quilt patches, we will fit together into a new pattern one day. It is in the hands of *le bon Dieu*.

Papa, too, has heard that a great war is coming between Britain and France. But he says it will end some day. Wars always do. He tells us Oncle Paul dreams of finding a new home in a French land called Louisiana. But Maman shook her head stubbornly when she heard that, and the rest of us feel as she does. When the war ends, we will not seek another strange land. We will return to Acadia!

Epilogue

The great war between Britain and France did come. It was called the Seven Years War, and it lasted from 1756 until 1763. These were hard times for Angélique and her family. To the people of Maryland and the other colonies, Acadians were the enemy, so they were not allowed to travel or meet in large groups. Many could not find enough work to support their families. But thanks to their own hard work and the help of Master Andrew Stygar, Angélique's family survived. Michel Richard, a skilled carpenter, was never short of work, and his sons worked with him. His wife Madeleine set up a laundry with the help of Madame Melanson and Jehanne. Some of the finest linens in Baltimore came to be washed and ironed in the house of the Acadians. As for Angélique, she rose from scullery maid to head parlour maid in the house of Master Hardcastle.

Through all those hard years, the Richards never stopped dreaming of the day they would return to Acadia. Every penny they could spare was set aside for their journey. As soon as the war ended, Michel and Angélique travelled to Oxford to see Paul Richard and his family. Angélique and Geneviève had a tearful reunion, but then their tongues wagged for days as they told each other everything that had happened to them. Meanwhile, Michel and Paul Richard were discussing the future. Plans were afoot for Acadians to journey to the colony of Louisiana, and Paul was determined to go. But Angélique's father stubbornly refused to give up the hope of returning to Acadia. At last, the two brothers said a fond farewell. Angélique never saw her cousin Geneviève again. On the way back to Baltimore, Michel and Angélique stopped at Annapolis to visit Belle's grave, and Angélique fulfilled her vow to plant a rosebush there. She and her father paid a visit to Mistress Finnerty, too, to thank her for all her kindnesses.

That same year, word came that Acadian families were gathering at Boston, Massachusetts, and were planning to walk back to Acadia. The Richards and the Melansons decided this was their chance. One of the last things Angélique did before leaving Baltimore was to cut a spring from her willow, which she had planted out behind the house of the Acadians. She potted it up and kept it moist on the journey.

The Richards and Melansons trekked from Baltimore to Boston, carrying their few belongings in a *charrette*. There they joined two hundred other families, and began their long journey north. Fearing the hatred of the New Englanders, the Acadians avoided main roads and kept to forest paths. For months they trudged onward, the women carrying children too small to walk, while the men pulled the carts. With no guns for hunting, they had to live on game they could trap or snare. The way was long and weary, with rugged mountains and swift rivers to cross. All suffered, and some died along the way, their graves marked by rough crosses in the wilderness. At last, after many trials, the survivors reached the mouth of the St. John River, where they met other Acadians who had settled there.

But bad news awaited them. Some who had already tried to return to Grand-Pré warned the Richards that all Acadian lands had been given to British settlers. There was no place for them in their former home. Heartbroken, the Richards at last gave up their dream of returning to Grand-Pré. Instead they and the Melansons decided to journey far up the St. John River, where other Acadians had found refuge from the British. There they took up land and began life again. Angélique planted her willow cutting, which grew and thrived, a living link with Old Acadia.

In their second spring on their new farm, a ragged, dusty figure appeared on the doorstep. It was Victor, who had held out against the British with Beausoleil until 1758. After that, the men had been imprisoned until the end of the war. Beausoleil then decided to go to Louisiana, but Victor had wandered far in search of his lost family until he found them at last. But neither he nor they ever learned the fate of Catherine.

The Melansons settled not far away from the Richards, so the two families were neighbours once more. Angélique and Jehanne had become friends at last, though they still argued sometimes. Jehanne soon married François Daigle, a distant cousin of Madeleine Richard's, and Angélique said that having a husband and children to order about all day long did wonders to soften Jehanne's tongue.

Angélique, however, refused all offers of marriage, believing it was her duty to remain at home to aid her mother. Madeleine Richard's health had become frail on their terrible journey north. But when Marie-Josèphe was old enough to be of real help to her mother, Angélique at last married Jean-Baptiste Melanson. So she and Jehanne became sisters. Jean-Baptiste vowed that he had loved Angélique since their first dance together at Catherine's wedding, and had waited patiently for her. Part of the small dowry Angélique brought to her new home was the quilt she had finally completed after many long years. Her first child was a daughter, whom Angélique named Cécile after her beloved sister. The girl inherited her aunt's beautiful blue eyes, and was always known as Belle. Angélique and Jean-Baptiste went on to have five more children, two girls and three boys.

When Marie-Josèphe married, her husband came to live on Michel and Madeleine's farm. Madeleine died in 1770, but Michel lived until 1775. Claude and Victor worked in the woods as lumberjacks during the winter and on the farm in the summer. Sometimes Claude would slip away downriver to spend a summer working at sea, returning with a light in his eyes and money in his pockets. He and Victor never married, and Victor remained the despair of single ladies until he was quite an old man.

In their old age, Angélique and her husband were lovingly cared for by Belle, and Angélique gave her the diary to pass down to her children. Angélique lived to be eighty-seven years old. She died in 1830, a year after Jean-Baptiste. In her last days, she loved to finger the squares in her quilt and tell her great-great-grandchildren the stories of each and every piece.

Angélique's willow grew into a large tree that was famous in all the country around. It became the custom for newlyweds to cut a sprig of it to plant for good luck.

Historical Note

Acadians are the descendants of the first French settlers in North America. The French colony of Port-Royal was founded in 1605, though a large number of settlers did not arrive until 1632. From the beginning the Acadians were caught up in the struggle of France and Britain to control North America. Port-Royal was not very far from the British colonies, and was frequently attacked by them and sometimes captured. As the Acadian population grew, new settlements were founded farther away, near Grand-Pré and the Isthmus of Chignecto. Acadians also settled in what are now the provinces of New Brunswick and Prince Edward Island.

In 1710, the British seized Port-Royal for good. Britain and France signed the Treaty of Utrecht in 1713. This granted the colony and all the territory then known as Nova Scotia to Britain — excluding Île Royale (Cape Breton) and Île Saint-Jean (Prince Edward Island). But the treaty left unclear where the western boundary of Nova Scotia was. France continued to claim the territory beyond the Isthmus of Chignecto, now known as New Brunswick. French troops remained in this area, and new French settlements were founded.

But what of the Acadians? The Treaty of Utrecht allowed them to stay in Nova Scotia if they would sign an oath of loyalty to the British king. This they at first refused to do. The French government wanted them to resettle in *la nouvelle Acadie française*, the area beyond the Isthmus of Chignecto. It sent agents such as the Abbé Le Loutre to persuade them. The British wanted the Acadians to leave, too.

Neither side counted on the stubbornness of the Acadians. They had worked hard to dike and reclaim marshlands to create their rich farms, and they believed they had a right to live in peace. Most Acadians saw no reason to leave. They wished to stay neutral in any future war.

For many years, the British did not bother the Acadians much. After all, the British government as yet had no settlers willing to populate Nova Scotia. Acadian crops were also a useful source of supply for British troops in the garrison at Port-Royal (now renamed Annapolis Royal). In 1730, the British tried again to get the Acadians to agree to fight against the French if war came, but the Acadians refused. In the end, they were allowed to sign a qualified oath of allegiance that did not require them to fight France. Governor Philips promised them verbally that they would never have to abandon their neutrality. However, Philips did not report this part of the agreement to his superiors. And the Acadians believed they had agreed to all that was necessary.

Throughout most of the 1740s, Britain and France were again at war. The French fortress of Louisbourg on Cape Breton Island was a danger to the British colonies, so in 1749 the British began to develop a rival fortress at Halifax. Settlers poured into the new colony, and suddenly the Acadians seemed a serious problem. If war broke out and they fought for France, they would be a danger to Halifax. The British government decided that the Acadians must sign an unconditional oath of loyalty. If not, they would have to leave Nova Scotia.

But the Acadians saw no reason to change their minds. Had they not been loyal for more than forty years? And had the British not threatened them before but done nothing? However, Charles Lawrence, the strong-willed new Governor of Nova Scotia, believed their neutrality was disloyalty. In 1755, Acadian delegates refused again to sign an unconditional oath. The governor ordered them to be deported.

The first deportations took place in 1755. By

the end of that year about half the 13,000 Acadians had been sent away. Hapless Acadian families, often separated in the confusion, were put on overcrowded ships. They were carried off to ports up and down the North American coast. Food and water ran short on many ships, and many people died on the journey. When the ships reached port, nobody wanted the Acadians. The colony of Virginia refused even to let them off the ships, which were sent on to England. Even when the Acadians were allowed ashore, few were lucky enough to find decent work. Many had to beg a living in order to save their children from starvation.

The terrible deportations did not end in 1755. Those left behind in Acadia were driven off their lands. Some fled to the French settlements along the St. Lawrence River. Others took to the woods. There they hid, starving in the winter cold. At last they were rounded up by British troops and deported. More Acadians escaped to the areas that are now New Brunswick and Prince Edward Island. But there was no refuge there, either. The French fortress of Louisbourg was captured by the British in 1758, and after that Acadians who were found anywhere were deported to England or France.

In 1763, after the end of the Seven Years War, the Acadians imprisoned in England were sent to France. In North America, a few managed to struggle back on foot to Nova Scotia. But their lands had been given to British settlers. They had to begin again in new settlements, on poor soil that no one else wanted to farm. Other Acadians settled in New Brunswick, at places like Caraquet and Tracadie. Still others had already made their way to the colony of Louisiana. After 1763, more Acadians went there by ship from the American colonies and France. One of these was Beausoleil Broussard, the Acadian hero. The descendants of the Acadians of Louisiana are known today as Cajuns.

In 1755, the British believed that by deporting the Acadians, they would destroy them as a people. But the Acadians survived, and after years of hardship they at last began to thrive again. Today, Acadian language and culture are stronger in Canada than ever. In 1994, 1999 and 2004 an Acadian World Congress has been held. In 2004 it was in Nova Scotia, marking the 400th anniversary of French settlement in North America.

Recently, certain groups of Acadians in the Maritime provinces and Louisiana have attempted to get an apology from the British Crown for the injustices committed during the deportation. In 2003, a Royal Proclamation from Britain, supported by the Government of Canada, was issued, acknowledging the sufferings of the Acadians during the expulsions. July 28, 2004, was designated as a special day to honour Canada's Acadian people.

An Acadian girl in typical dress.

The rolling meadows of Grand-Pré near the mouth of the Gaspereau.

An ongoing job in the lives of Acadian farmers was building and repairing the dikes that were such a feature of the Grand Pré landscape.

The reading of the order of expulsion to the Acadians in the parish church at Grand Pré in 1755.

Gentlemen:

I have received from his Excellency Governor Lawrence, the King's Commission which I have in my hand and by whose orders you are convened together to Manifest to you his Majesty's final resolution to the French inhabitants of this his Province of Nova Scotia who for almost half a century have had more indulgence granted them, than any of his subjects in any part of his Dominions. What use you have made of them you yourself best know.

The part of duty I am now upon is what though necessary is very disagreeable to my nature make and temper, as I know it must be grievous to you who are of the same specie.

But it is not my business to animadvert, but to obey such orders as I receive and therefore without hesitation shall deliver you his Majesty's orders and instructions viz.

That your lands and tenements, cattle of all kinds and livestock of all sorts are forfeited to the Crown with all other your effects saving your money and household goods and you yourselves to be removed from this his province.

Thus it is peremptorily his Majesty's orders that the whole French inhabitants of these districts, be removed, and I am through his Majesty's goodness, directed to allow you liberty to carry of your money and household goods as many as you

> can without discommoding the vessels you go in. I shall do everything in my power that all those goods be secured to you and that you are not molested in carrying them and also that whole families shall go in the same vessel and make this remove which I am sensible must give you a great deal of trouble as easy as his Majesty's service will admit and hope that in what every part of the world you may fall, you may be faithful subjects, a peaceable and happy people.
>
> I must also inform you that it is his Majesty's pleasure that you remain in security under the inspection and Direction of the troops that I have the Honour to command.

An excerpt from the Deportation Proclamation, 1755. Though some attempt was made to keep families together, many were separated and sent to different ports on different ships.

Colonel John Winslow, who was in charge of removing the Acadians from Grand Pré.

Acadian families were forced out of their homes and had their buildings burned.

Acadian families wait on shore, huddled with their possessions, before being forced aboard British ships.

The chapel that stands at the Grand Pré National Park today, at the site of the original Acadian church. The statue of Evangeline, a fictional Acadian girl who was immortalized in Henry Wadsworth Longfellow's poem, was built by two sculptors of Acadian descent and unveiled in 1920.

Longfellow depicted the tragedy of the Acadian expulsion in his story-length poem, Evangeline, *first published in 1847. The poem helped bring the plight of the Acadians to the attention of the world.*

A photograph of Grand Pré today.

The Deportation Cross, at the site where the Acadians boarded the ships in 1755. Because the shoreline has changed over the centuries, the cross now stands farther inland.

Glossary of French Words

au fond: in fact, after all
boucherie: community butchering
charivari: noise-making outside newlyweds' window
charrette: oxcart or two-wheeled cart
chez: at the home of
la douce France: traditional term for France

en arrière: go back
fête: feast
fraises sauvages: wild strawberries
fricot: thick soup or stew
grâce au bon Dieu: thanks to the good Lord
grande corvée: gathering for work, such as a
   quilting "bee"
grande fête: big celebration
grand'prée: great diked meadow
grenier: attic
hélas: alas
maudits Anglais: confounded English
la nouvelle Acadie: New Acadia, the lands beyond
   the Isthmus of Chignecto
pauvre: poor
plus tard: later
porc-épic: porcupine
première neige de mai: first snow of May, thought
   to have healing properties
pour sûr: sure enough
quelle surprise: what a surprise
ragoût: stew
sabots: wooden shoes
tant pis: too bad
tisane: medicinal solution
veillée: evening gathering

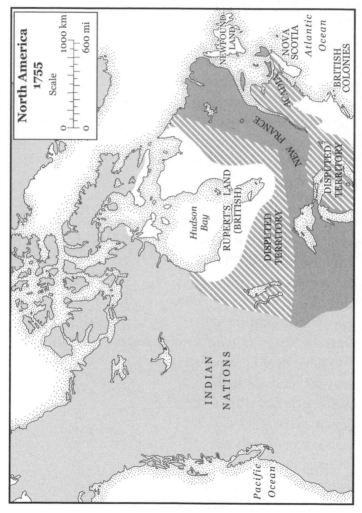

Acadia was a rich land long claimed by both the French and the British.

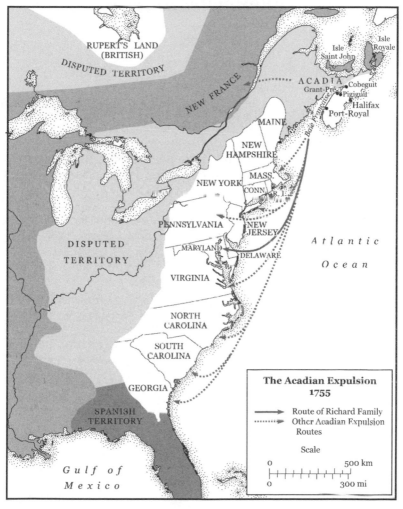

In what has been called "le grand dérangement," Acadians were sent as far away as Georgia and England.

Acknowledgments

Grateful acknowledgment is made for permission to reprint the following:

Cover portrait: Detail from Otto Jacobi, *Portrait of a Girl, 1862*, courtesy of Musée des Beaux-Arts de Montréal.
Cover background: Detail (lightened) from Parks Canada, *Le départ vers l'exil, 1755*, by Claude Picard, H-03-08-01-00(D4).

Page 182: National Library of Canada, WOB84165.
Page 183: E.B. Schell, from *Picturesque Canada*, Vol. II, National Archives of Canada, C-085544.
Page 184: *Repairing a dyke*, History Collection, Nova Scotia Museum, painted by Azor Viennau.
Page 185: C.W. Jefferys, *Reading the order of expulsion to the Acadians in the parish church at Grand Pré, in 1755*, National Archives of Canada, C-73709.
Pages 186–187: Excerpt from the Deportation Proclamation.
Page 187 (lower): C.W. Jefferys, General John Winslow, National Archives of Canada, C-69902.
Page 188: *Burning and Lay Waste* by Claude Picard; © Parks Canada, 03 08 01 00 05.
Page 189: Parks Canada, *Le départ vers l'exil, 1755*, (cropped), by Claude Picard, H-03-08-01-00(D4).
Page 190: François Gaudet, photograph of the Grand Pré Parks Canada site and the Evangeline statue.
Page 191 (upper): James Faed, *Evangeline*, courtesy of University of Moncton.

Page 191 (lower): François Gaudet, photograph of the Grand Pré Parks Canada site.

Page 192 (upper): Deportation Cross, photograph by Carrie MacDonald, courtesy of Bruce Fuller.

Pages 194–195: Maps by Paul Heersink/Paperglyphs. Map data © 2002 Government of Canada with permission from Natural Resources Canada.

Thanks to Barbara Hehner for her careful checking of the manuscript, and to Dr. Neil Bouchard, Vice-president Academic and former Professor of Acadian History at Université Sainte Anne in Nova Scotia, for generously sharing his expertise.

To the memory of my mother,
Lucille Agathe Lépine,
whose Acadian heritage is the inspiration
for this story.
And to Roderick, for all the reasons.

About the Author

Sharon Stewart had known that there were Acadians on her mother's side of the family, but until she began to write *Banished from Our Home*, she didn't realize how true that family legend was. There had always been an oral tradition that the Lépines — her mother's family — were partly descended from Acadians, though direct knowledge of the connection had been lost. There was also a story that at least one distant relative had ended up in Louisiana following the deportations.

Sharon had not followed up on the family story until she began researching Angélique's story. It was then that the surprises began cropping up. "A distant cousin had just completed a Lépine family tree going back into the seventeenth century, and the Acadian connection was there, through a Euphrosine Maheu, born at Port-Royal, who had ended up in Quebec after the deportations. She was descended from an Angélique Richard born in 1696 in Acadia. So that's why I decided to give my heroine the name Angélique Richard." Sharon was also excited to discover a family land grant at Port-Royal shown in the *Historical Atlas of Canada.* "It's one thing to read genealogical charts, but quite another to see the actual spot where family members homesteaded so long ago." Branches of the family later settled at Grand Pré and at Beaubassin, near the Isthmus of Chignecto.

In searching out her roots, Sharon discovered another cousin, François Gaudet, whose photographs appear on pages 190–191. Finding out about these relatives, she says, "made me appreciate how much Acadians were and are one big family. There were relatively few people, especially in the early years of the colony, so everyone intermarried with everyone else. This made the deportation that much more cruel. Because even if immediate families were deported together, people were torn from their web of belonging. It must have been unimaginably horrible."

In 1755, the Richards from whom Sharon is descended were scattered to the four winds, like many other Acadians. Some of them were sent to Maryland, and others to England and later on to France. After the Seven Years War, some Richards settled in Louisiana. Today the family proudly call themselves *les Richards de partout* — the Richards of everywhere.

Though of course the Richards in *Banished from Our Home* are fictional, the character of

Angélique is based to some extent on Sharon's mother, Lucille Agathe Lépine. "She had a sister named Eugénie Cécile, whom she teased by calling her Eugénie Sausage. Another sister, Eva, was always called Belle, especially by my grandfather. My mother confessed to being envious of Belle's good looks."

Sharon has done graduate work in French colonial history, of which Acadia was a part, so she knew a good deal about the deportations. And she had also visited Grand Pré, so she was acquainted with the locale of the story. Those threads, and of course the family legend, weave together in *Banished from Our Home*.

One of Sharon's earlier books, *The Dark Tower*, depicts the era of the French revolution and the dramatic story of a princess that history forgot, Marie Thérèse Charlotte of France. That book was shortlisted for the both the Red Cedar Award and the Geoffrey Bilson Award for Historical Fiction. She has also written about the Russian revolution in *My Anastasia* (also shortlisted for the Red Cedar Award), a moving story of Russia's last duchess. But Sharon's writing is not limited to historical fiction. Her most recent book is a soaring adventure, *Raven Quest*. Her other books are *The Minstrel Boy*, a novel with echoes of

Arthurian times, *Spider's Web*, a story about the Internet, and *City of the Dead*, a book of stories that blend mythology, technology and the unexpected. *City of the Dead* was shortlisted for both the Red Maple and Snow Willow awards.

Copyright © 2004 by Sharon Stewart.

All rights reserved. Published by Scholastic Canada Ltd.
SCHOLASTIC and DEAR CANADA and logos are trademarks
and/or registered trademarks of Scholastic Inc.

National Library of Canada Cataloguing in Publication

Stewart, Sharon (Sharon Roberta), 1944-
Banished from our home : the Acadian diary of Angélique Richard /
Sharon Stewart.

ISBN 0-439-97421-6

1. Acadians--Expulsion, 1755--Juvenile fiction. I. Title.

PS8587.T4895B35 2004   jC813'.54   C2004-900880-3

No part of this publication may be reproduced or stored in a retrieval
system, or transmitted in any form or by any means, electronic,
mechanical, recording, or otherwise, without written permission of the
publisher, Scholastic Canada Ltd., 175 Hillmount Road, Markham,
Ontario L6C 1Z7, Canada. In the case of photocopying or other
reprographic copying, a licence must be obtained from Access Copyright
(Canadian Copyright Licensing Agency), 1 Yonge Street, Suite 1900,
Toronto, Ontario M5E 1E5 (1 800-893-5777).

6 5 4 3 2 1 Printed in Canada 04 05 06 07 08

The display type was set in CalligraphyFLF.
The text was set in Esprit Book.

Printed in Canada
First printing June 2004

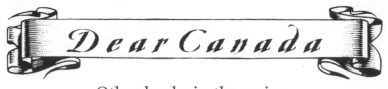

Other books in the series:

A Prairie as Wide as the Sea
The Immigrant Diary of Ivy Weatherall
by Sarah Ellis

Orphan at My Door
The Home Child Diary of Victoria Cope
by Jean Little

With Nothing But Our Courage
The Loyalist Diary of Mary MacDonald
by Karleen Bradford

Footsteps in the Snow
The Red River Diary of Isobel Scott
by Carol Matas

A Ribbon of Shining Steel
The Railway Diary of Kate Cameron
by Julie Lawson

Whispers of War
The War of 1812 Diary of Susanna Merritt
by Kit Pearson